COW PATTY
A JUSTICE SECURITY NOVEL
By
T. M. Bilderback

Copyright 2015 By T. M. Bilderback

Chapter 1

The big commercial jet set down at the airport in Carson City, Nevada. The big wheels "*skwerped*" twice, then settled down. The pilots engaged the brakes, and the plane slowed down considerably. Finally, it taxied to a stop at boarding gate number seven.

Patty Ferguson and Brandon King gathered their carry-on bags, and stepped into the aisle. They were taking a couple of weeks off from Justice Security, and enjoying a vacation in the city that they had visited only once before – when one of the Justice Security private jets had been shot down by a rogue stealth fighter. On that earlier visit, as they left the hotel to return home, Brandon had gambled a dollar in the cheap hotel's one-armed bandit, and had hit the one hundred thousand dollar jackpot. He promptly split the money fifty-fifty with Patty. She and Brandon were best friends, and, besides, he had borrowed the dollar from her, anyway.

The vacation was a stress reliever. After being promoted to plain clothes, they both had been told that they'd be going to the top secret second Justice Security location. The second location was being constructed from the ground up, and the work was being overseen by Justice Security's new partner, Jim Dandy. He would be the main partner that they answered to, but, supposedly, the company was going to court another person as a partner to assist with the new location. The second site was basically a hideaway, should everyone be forced by circumstances to go to ground. Its location was top secret.

Patty and Brandon, before reporting to the new location, had asked for a vacation. They had both liked Carson City – what little they had seen of it, anyway – and wanted to come back. And not just because of the money that Brandon had won.

Patty had found the desert comforting. And that was surprising, because she wasn't an outdoor person.

As they made their way through the airport, Patty asked Brandon where he had made hotel reservations.

3

"Big Daddy's Hotel."

Patty stopped walking. "You're kidding, right?"

Brandon stopped, too. "No. It was rated five stars by people at that online place."

Shaking her head, Patty began walking again. "Big Daddy's. Wow. Only you, Brandon."

"What's wrong with Big Daddy's?"

"I may be surprised, but it's probably a dump. Or a brothel."

"Such negativity. You're the one that harped at me for dropping that dollar into the one-armed bandit. Look how that turned out."

"I know. Brandon, you're an ass!"

"Trust me on this, will you?"

"Okay, but it better be good."

Brandon shrugged. "If it turns out to be a brothel, at least you can make a little money while we're there."

Patty almost hit him with her purse, but he ducked in time.

"Asshole!"

Brandon was smiling. "Remember that guy in high school? The one that confessed that he wanted to smear peanut butter all over you?"

Patty shuddered. "Ewww, Brandon!"

"Then there was that college guy you dated for a while...what was his name? Biff? Burke?"

They were at the luggage carousel now.

"Brock." Patty snagged her light blue suitcase.

"Oh, yeah, Brock. The fraternity man. Phi Beta Delta, wasn't he? After two dates, he asked if you'd pull a train for the fraternity."

"I kicked his ass."

Brandon laughed as he grabbed his red suitcase. "You did. Right in front of his fraternity brothers. I think his voice is still high-pitched from where you kicked him. And it wasn't his ass, it was his..."

"Why are you bringing all this up?"

"I'm just saying, if it *is* a brothel, you know how to tell them to go screw *themselves*. And can kick their asses if they don't."

Patty smiled and shook her head at her best friend.

"You are totally nuts, Brandon King."

"Of course I am. That's why you love me so much. That, and I always let you have the good crayons."

Patty and Brandon had been best friends since kindergarten. He had stood by her side through the tough classes, puberty, and the nightmare that had been high school. She had stood by his side through all of the same things, and supported him when he told his parents that he was gay. They had watched each other's backs ever since. Both were offered promotions to plain clothes within Justice Security earlier, and both had turned them down for two reasons. They both felt that they weren't ready, and neither one would accept it until the other got promoted, too. Patty and Brandon stuck together, through thick and thin.

But, now they were ready, and had accepted the promotions. And they were very proud of them.

They were outside the airport now, standing in the bright, hot sunshine. Patty's fair complexion stood out so much in the sunlight that she almost seemed to glow. Her blonde hair fluttered in the light breeze, and the freckles that were lightly scattered across her cheeks and the bridge of her nose caught the sunlight, and drank it in. She closed her eyes and turned her face toward the sun.

Brandon stood beside her, looking around for a taxi. Both had their suitcases on the sidewalk beside them.

"Brandon?"

"What?"

"Will I ever find Mr. Right?"

Brandon smiled. "Of course you will, Patty. And I'll be so very envious."

She turned to her friend and smiled. "How about you and Chris? Have you spoken to him since he moved out?"

Brandon shook his head. "No. I guess he really didn't love me." He looked at her. "He did tell me that, you know."

Patty shook her head. "No, I didn't. You didn't mention that to me."

Brandon looked away, and nodded. "Yeah. He said that I wasn't there enough for him. He said that I spent too much time at work."

Patty nodded. "We *do* spend a lot of time at work, don't we?"

"We do. And he said something else."

"What?"

Brandon sighed. "He said that he wasn't going to risk his love on someone that could be killed any minute."

Patty looked outraged. "But that can happen anywhere! With any job!"

"Most jobs don't involve the Giambinis, or Esteban Fernandez, or rogue senators, either."

A taxi had pulled up to them. The driver got out and opened the trunk for their suitcases.

"Welcome to Carson City, folks! Where to?"

As they put their suitcases into the taxi's trunk, Patty said, "Big Daddy's, please."

The driver nodded. "Nice choice."

"Why do you say that?" asked Brandon.

"Big Daddy's is one nice hotel. Nice, honest casino, too." He climbed in behind the wheel inside the air-conditioned car.

Patty looked at Brandon. "Just watch. It's a brothel."

Brandon laughed at his friend as they got into the car.

BIG DADDY'S WAS NOT a brothel.

According to the taxi driver, it was rumored that pressure had been applied to Homer Crenshaw, the "Big Daddy" that the hotel was named after, to add that service to the hotel's offerings. Homer had flatly refused. The people that had applied pressure were people that usually didn't like to hear the word 'no'. Homer expressed his concerns to the Carson City Sheriff's Office, and his complaint was duly registered. The Sheriff's Office told him that without a name connected to the person or persons that had applied pressure, even though a good description had been provided, there wasn't much that could be done about the complaint. Homer had been on pins and needles ever since.

"How do you know all of this?" Brandon's question to the taxi driver was incredulous.

The driver glanced at Brandon in the rear-view mirror, and smiled. "Come on, son! You know priests, taxi drivers, hookers, and maids all know the best gossip! People talk around us like we aren't there. We *all* know stuff like that."

Brandon nodded. "Good to know. Thanks."

The taxi pulled into the drive for Big Daddy's.

The driver said, "Well, here we are, kids. And, if you two are the two that I think you are, Big Daddy himself is probably waiting for you."

Patty and Brandon exchanged puzzled looks.

"We're just a couple of folks on vacation, buddy," said Patty.

The driver turned around and looked at them. "Uh-huh." He turned back and got out of the car, opened the passenger door beside Brandon, and then popped the trunk.

The two vacationers hopped out of the taxi and went around to collect their bags. Once they had, the driver closed the trunk, shut the passenger door, and told them, "Good luck!" just before climbing into the taxi and driving away.

The hotel valet that came to carry their luggage was dressed in jeans, a western-looking shirt, and a tan, big-brimmed cowboy hat. His name tag read, "Slim". When he walked up to them, he said, "Howdy, sir...ma'am," and tipped his hat slightly to Patty. "Welcome to Big Daddy's, the best darn *ho*-tel in these parts! If you folks'll follow me, I'll take you right to the front desk!"

Sharing a smile between them at Slim's good nature, the two vacationing friends followed the man into the lobby.

The hotel lobby was set up to resemble the main room of an old western ranch, with a huge fireplace, and a set of longhorn steer horns over the mantle. There were several comfortable-looking leather chairs, love seats, and couches arranged throughout the lobby, with small tables here and there. A wagon wheel chandelier hung from the ceiling, with frosted lantern shades covering the lightbulbs. An old saddle hung from the ceiling, along with various pieces of livery. The main desk was built to resemble a western hotel desk, complete with pigeonholed message boxes behind the reception area. Each pigeonhole was labeled with a room number, and electronic key cards were inside each one.

Two desk clerks worked behind the hotel desk. Both were women, and were dressed in western outfits. One wore jeans and a denim shirt, and the other wore what looked like a suede skirt that reached just below her knees. Her shirt was white cotton. Both wore cowboy hats. The woman in the skirt was working with a customer, so Slim directed Patty and Brandon to the woman in jeans.

The woman, whose name tag read, "Jenny", looked up at them and smiled a bright, pretty smile. "Howdy, folks! Welcome to Big Daddy's! Do you have reservations?"

Brandon quipped, "No, we really want to stay here."

Jenny laughed a polite laugh while Patty rolled her eyes at her friend.

"Brandon, shut up!" said Patty, trying to look fierce.

"That look stopped working on me in sixth grade, girl," Brandon replied.

Patty shook her head. "Man. Jenny, why does my best friend embarrass me that way?"

Jenny shrugged, as if to say 'I don't know, and I'm not getting into the middle of this one.'

Patty smiled. "Patty Ferguson and Brandon King. Two rooms, please, or a suite with two bedrooms."

Jenny typed their names into her computer. "Yes, I have you. Oh, I have a note beside your names." She read the note, raised her eyebrows, and said, "Your rooms have been comped, by Big Daddy himself. He also has a request to be notified when you arrive, and that he would like very much to meet you." She looked them both over after she said the last sentence, as if she were trying to see what was so special about the two young people that made her boss want to meet with them.

Both Patty and Brandon looked surprised when they heard what Jenny had to say. Patty turned to Brandon.

"Have you done something I need to know about?"

Brandon shook his head. "I'm as clueless as you are, Patty. I just booked the rooms online for two weeks. Never spoke to a soul."

Jenny had picked up the hotel phone and was now whispering quietly into it. She placed it back on its receiver and spoke to Slim. "They're in the VIP suite, Slim, if you want to take their bags on up." She looked at Patty and Brandon. "Big Daddy would like to see you. Would you please follow me?"

Brandon shrugged. "Sure. Why not?"

Slim left with their bags, presumably to take them to the young people's suite. Jenny walked to the end of the reception desk, into a room that obviously was for staff only. There was a door in the wall beside the desk that had a sign that read, "WHOA, pardner! Staff only 'round here!". The door opened, and Jenny motioned the two inside.

"Please follow me," repeated Jenny.

The door opened into a small vestibule that contained a long hallway with dark paneling and timbers crossing the ceiling. Closed doors were spaced along the hallway, but Jenny was ignoring each of these. She stopped at the end of the hall at a set of double oak doors, with ornate hinges, locks, and antique glass doorknobs. A sign hung from the door. Burned into the sign's wood was the name "Homer Crenshaw".

Jenny knocked on one of the double doors, and opened it without waiting for a response. She stood to one side to allow Patty and Brandon to enter the room first.

It was an extravagant room. Real wood paneling, very dark, covered the walls, and the ceiling was vaulted with wood timbers marching across. A huge crystal chandelier draped down from the center of the ceiling. A huge mahogany desk faced the doors, and leather seats were arranged in front of and facing it. The desktop was very Spartan, with only a desk phone and a lamp visible. A huge leather executive chair rested behind the desk. A wet bar was located on the left of the entry door, complete with a normal-sized refrigerator. A gun cabinet was on the right wall. The cabinet contained several rifles, shotguns, and handguns displayed behind glass, and all of them were hanging on wooden dowels imbedded in the back, and unobtrusive lighting gleamed from each weapon. Another fireplace, not quite as large as the lobby fireplace, rested against the left wall of the huge office, and a leather couch and two leather recliners were placed in front of the fireplace. The requisite longhorn steer horns were displayed above the fireplace, and several Native American rugs with beautiful intricate patterns adorned the walls.

Strolling around from behind the mahogany desk was a man, presumably Crenshaw. He was six feet tall, and wore jeans and a western-type shirt, a string tie, and a cowboy hat and boots. He was approximately fifty years old, and looked tanned, healthy, and very strong. He was smiling broadly, displaying white teeth, and he meant the smile, because it actually touched his eyes as well as his mouth.

"Welcome to Big Daddy's! I'm so pleased to meet ya'll! I'm Homer Crenshaw, but ya'll can call me Big Daddy!" His good nature was not lost on Brandon and Patty, and both shook his hand vigorously as they returned the smiles. As he shook Patty's hand, he said, "Hot dang, ain't you 'bout the purtiest thing I've seen in a long while! If I was your daddy, I'd keep a shotgun loaded with rock salt handy to keep the men off of ya!"

Patty blushed happily. "Thank you, Mr. Cren...I mean, Big Daddy."

Crenshaw's smiled widened. "Darlin', you can just call me Daddy! You're like the daughter I wish I had!"

Crenshaw turned to Brandon. "Son, you look sharp! I hear you're the one that hit the jackpot at Old Man Bumpus's hotel last month! That old coot didn't think that machine would ever pay off! He's talking like he might have to shut down the hotel just cause he had to pay out on that winner! Congratulations, son! Good job!"

Brandon smiled like an idiot.

Crenshaw put his hands together at chest level, and then moved them toward the young people. "I bet ya'll are wonderin' why I wanted to talk to you, ain't ya?"

Both Brandon and Patty nodded.

"Well, let me tell ya...wait, where's my manners? Ya'll want somethin' to drink? You name it, I got it...right over there on that bar."

Patty smiled demurely, and answered for both of them. "No, thank you, Mr. Cren...I mean, *Daddy*. We're just ready to start our vacations."

Crenshaw nodded and nodded. "I *know* ya'll are, and I'm sorry to keep you from it. Please sit down, both of you." He gestured to two of the leather chairs across from his desk.

The two vacationers sat down, Brandon on the left and Patty on the right. Crenshaw, still smiling, walked around the desk to his own chair, sat down, and then tilted back and propped his boot-encased feet on the corner of his desk.

"Look, I'll be honest Injun with you two. I did some research on you, when that online reservation came in. You had listed Justice Security as your employers, and everybody's heard of them, even way out here in Carson City. Now, you might not believe this, but I've got a small problem."

Brandon cleared his throat. "Actually, we may know about your problem, sir." He explained to Crenshaw about the taxi driver's story.

"Shucks, son, that's only part of it," replied Crenshaw. "Those fellers have been inside my casino twice, and on the property more than that. I keep runnin' 'em off, but they keep comin' back."

"And the sheriff isn't any help to you?" asked Patty.

"I file complaint after complaint, and the sheriff doesn't do anything. I believe he's got his hand in their pocket pretty deep. Wouldn't matter if he didn't have his hands out for their cash – bastard couldn't find his own ass with both hands and a flashlight."

Patty and Brandon exchanged a look. Brandon shrugged. Patty looked back at Crenshaw.

"Big Daddy, why exactly are you telling us all of this?" said Patty.

"Oh, I thought you knew! I want to hire you to protect my interests! Ever-body knows Justice Security's reputation, and it would be such a favor to me if you'd help!"

"Sir, you *do* realize that Patty and I are on vacation, right?" asked Brandon.

"I sure do, son! It wouldn't be a *formal* thing, see…I'd just let word sneak out that Justice Security has a couple of people here in the hotel to keep out…well, let's say head off any trouble. I wouldn't expect ya'll to do much, just normal stuff anybody else would do! You can use the pool, or gamble some in the casino…hell, I'll even front ya'll ten grand to play with! Just so you kinda hang around…as kind of a deterrent. Know what I mean?"

The two looked at each other. Brandon shrugged, as if to say, 'I don't care. It's up to you.' Patty nodded slightly at him, and he nodded back. They had been friends for so long that they had a complete conversation without saying a word.

Patty took out her cell phone. "Big Daddy, we'll do it, as long as we can sell our bosses on it. Let me set up a 'face' call, and you can explain it to them."

"Sounds like a plan to me, darlin'!"

JIM DANDY WAS SITTING in on the nine o'clock meeting at the Justice Security building in the city. He still couldn't get used to the fact that he was now not only *working* for Justice Security, but a full-fledged *partner* in the company.

For years, after a falling out with Joey Justice back in college over Misty Wilhite, Jim had run a competing security company, Jim Dandy Security. He would snicker with glee every time he outbid Justice Security on a job, but Jim never had the success that his former friends had found with Justice Security.

Then, a couple of weeks earlier, Jim had received some information from an old acquaintance showing that Esteban Fernandez had been paying off someone high up in the United States Government. After one of Justice Security's private jets had been shot down in the Mojave Desert, and Jim, along with Marcus Moore, Joey Justice, and Misty Wilhite, had bailed out of an airplane that was heading to D. C. and was piloted by two assassins, they had found out who was behind it all. The FBI's arrest of the Chairman of the Senate Intelligence Committee, and the overwhelming evidence that Justice Security presented, had put Justice Security in the eyes of the entire country. Of course, the senator had not lasted long at all in prison. Esteban Fernandez had seen to that, and that prison murder was still headlining cable news outlets across the world.

During that adventure, the building housing Jim's rival company had been torched by the two assassins that hijacked their plane, so Joey and Jim had buried their problems, rekindled their friendship, and brought Jim Dandy Security under the Justice Security banner. Jim was to be in charge of the construction of a duplicate building in a top-secret location, so that Justice Security could use it as a hideaway to escape to if they ever needed it.

But, today, Jim was still learning procedures, and the nine o'clock meeting every morning was one of them. Since he would be at a remote location, Jim would be reporting by secure internet connections every morning. On the off chance that he simply couldn't report, his executive secretary, Emily Owens, would participate in the morning meeting.

Jim looked around the round conference table in the situation room.

Jessica Queen still had faded bruises on her face, and her arm was still in a cast. She had a few more weeks until her broken arm healed.

Percival "King Louie" Washington was scheduled to have the stitches taken out of the cut on his head later that morning. His concussion was gone.

Dr. Orville Eugene "Call me Buddy" Bishop, the Justice Security staff physician that Joey had stolen from the FBI, had repeatedly told both partners how lucky they were to have only the minor injuries that they had. He said that if Captain Trotter, the pilot of the private jet that had been shot down, had not been as capable as she had demonstrated, the injuries would have been much worse, if not fatal. As it was, they had lost the copilot of the jet, and that loss haunted all of them deeply. Dr. Bishop had issued a prescription for all three survivors of the jet: Set up appointments with Dr. Caleb Mitchell, the Justice Security staff psychiatrist. None of them could return to work without Dr. Mitchell's okay.

Marcus Moore, the FBI liaison to Justice Security, had broken his leg in the jump from the other plane. The four of them had two parachutes between them, and it had been a very close thing. Misty had fallen from the plane without a chute, Marcus had not had a secure grip on her when his chute deployed, and Jim had managed to catch her at the last minute with the other parachute. Joey had jumped from the plane last, blown it up with a flare, and used an emergency raft to slow his descent and help him angle his fall so that he caught up with Marcus. When Marcus and Joey had landed together, Marcus had not unlocked his knee in time, and his leg had broken.

Marcus, who got airsick at the mere thought of being on a plane, now added one more reason to avoid flying whenever possible.

Jim glanced at Dexter Beck. He was snuggled close to his wife Megan, and they were the operators of the secure setup that Joey and Misty were using at the moment. They were speaking with Charlie Li.

Charlie Li had relieved Jessica at her post during the Chicago mission. Jessica had taken on the job as head of security for the super-popular actress, Carly Stewart. Carly had difficulty remaining sober, and would happily use anything that crossed her path that would keep her intoxicated. When Charlie took over, he had fallen in love with the actress, and they had eloped to Reno. The tabloids reported that Carly had passed out immediately after saying 'I do', but the marriage apparently was a happy one between them.

In other words, Charlie had not had enough. Not yet.

But the stress of living with a drug-using alcoholic was beginning to show in the lines of his face. The dark circles under his eyes showed just how little sleep he had been getting.

"Is it really that bad, Charlie?" asked Misty quietly.

Charlie looked weary. "You have no idea, Misty."

"I do," said Jessica. "I spent lots of time with her. I have a working knowledge of the situation, believe me."

"Charlie, what can we do to help you?" asked Joey.

Charlie's lips thinned. He looked directly into his computer's camera. "I want to send her to rehab. It might be against her will, but, as her husband, I can do that, can't I?"

Joey looked skeptical. "I'm really not sure, Charlie. I'll have to check with Caleb on this one, and get back to you." Joey rubbed his cheeks with his hands. "Justice Security would be glad to foot the bill for you...that's not the issue. Putting her into rehab without her consent? Especially a star like Carly?" He shook his head. "I'm not sure how that will work out. But, I'll certainly do my best!"

Charlie smiled slightly into the camera. "Thank you, Joey."

Joey smiled back. "Not a problem, Charlie. Glad to help out. I'll call you after I've talked to Caleb."

"Thanks."

The discussion was terminated.

Joey turned back to the table. "Okay, does anyone else have anything?"

Jim's cell phone rang. He looked at the caller, and told the group, "It's Patty. Maybe we should hold on for a moment." He pressed the answer button. "Hello, Patty, what's wrong? I thought you and Brandon were on vacation!" He listened for a minute, and then said, "Wait a minute...let me put you on speaker." He touched the correct buttons, and the call went to speaker. "Okay, all of us are here. Can you start over?"

"Sure, Jim. I called you because Joey said that you're the man we mainly answer to, so I need to throw this at you." Patty explained everything that she had been told, and what Crenshaw wanted. "So, before I committed for Justice Security, I thought I'd better ask for permission."

"Patty, is Mr. Crenshaw with you right now?" asked Dexter.

"Yes, sir, he is."

"Okay, hold on...I'm going to switch to "face time" on Jim's phone, and hook it up so that we can all see each other."

Dexter plugged a cord into Jim's phone. He tapped a few keys on the keyboard in front of him, and Patty's face was suddenly on every monitor in the room.

Almost to himself, Dexter said, "*There* you are." He looked up at the monitor. "Patty, can you see all of us?"

Patty smiled. "I sure can, sir."

Joey said, "Would you please put Mr. Crenshaw on speaker and in front of the phone's camera?"

Patty tapped the proper buttons on her phone. "Okay, you're on speaker, and Mr. Crenshaw is right here."

The picture on the monitors moved as Patty handed off her phone, and Homer Crenshaw's face filled the screens.

A big smile crossed Crenshaw's face. "Well, howdy, folks! I sure didn't expect to talk to such a big group of folks!"

Joey smiled at Crenshaw. "Hello, Mr. Crenshaw. Let me make sure that I understand what you're asking. You'd like Brandon and Patty to work with you...let's say, *undercover*, for the two weeks of their stay?"

"Well, like I told 'em, it's not really working so much as it is just bein' here. As kind of a deterrent to any shenanigans that may crop up."

"So you really don't want them to do anything, except to hang around. And maybe spread the word that two Justice Security people just *happen* to be on the premises. Is that it?" asked Joey.

"That sums it up about right," replied Crenshaw.

Joey smirked. "And for this, you'll do...what?"

"Why, I'd give 'em the best suite in the house, *gratis*, and give 'em ten grand of house credit to play with in the casino."

Everyone around the table either smiled or chuckled quietly to themselves.

"Mr. Crenshaw, would you ask the kids to come into camera range, please?" asked Misty.

"Of course, ma'am."

The partners could hear some off-camera talking, and then Patty and Brandon appeared on the monitor.

"Okay, kids, you heard what the man wants, right?" asked Joey.

"Yes, sir," said Brandon.

"Basically, Mr. Crenshaw is offering you a free stay at his hotel and casino so that he can say that he has Justice Security on the premises. It pays for your hotel room, and some casino fun. You two are officially on vacation, so the decision is yours. We're okay with it here."

Both young people smiled into the phone's camera.

"We'll be glad to do it, Joey. It sounds like a really difficult case, but I think we can handle it," said Patty, smiling.

Louie spoke up. "Patty-girl, don't say things like that. You'll jinx yourself."

Jessica added, "Louie's right. It might come back and bite you on your arse."

Chapter 2

Two days later, Patty was reclining in one of the chaise lounge chairs beside the enormous swimming pool. Brandon was on the diving board, preparing to cannonball into the pool once again in a vain attempt to splash her.

No one else was using the pool.

Brandon ran, and bounced as hard as he could on the end of the diving board. His momentum carried him about six feet into the air. He brought his legs up to his chest, and bent his head so that it was between his knees. He hit the water hard, and, unfortunately, his testicles hit the water first. When he surfaced, he was yelling.

"Ow! Ow! Ow! Oh, my *God*, that *hurts*!"

Patty couldn't help herself. She burst out laughing.

"Oh, sure, laugh it up, Paleface! I may have ruined my masculinity trying to get you wet!"

Patty laughed even harder at Brandon's choice of wording.

Brandon climbed out of the pool and walked stiffly over to the chaise beside Patty. He sat down slowly, wincing with effort.

"I'm so glad my manly ruination is giving you pleasure!"

Patty started another round of hard laughing.

Brandon tried to maintain his composure, but he soon lost it. He began laughing too.

Finally, when the two couldn't laugh any more, Patty said, "Are you okay now?"

Brandon smiled at his best friend. "Yeah, I'm all right."

"This has been a wonderful couple of days, hasn't it?"

"Very relaxing. I'm glad we came here. I like this place."

After the phone call home, Patty and Brandon had again been welcomed by Big Daddy Crenshaw, and profusely thanked for their playing their part. He even told them that he'd comp their meals, too, if they would take a look at their hotel security, and offer a couple of pointers. Brandon took him up on it, since either of them could have done it. Brandon accompanied Crenshaw, while Patty was shown to their suite.

And a beautiful suite it was.

It contained a tastefully decorated, well-furnished sitting room, with an alcove for a small kitchenette. A door was located on the left and the right of the suite, and behind each door was a large, fully-furnished bedroom. Each bedroom contained western-styled king-sized beds, and were extremely comfortable...and they also contained a dresser with mirror, two nightstands, a closet, two armchairs, and dressing chair. Each bedroom also contained its own luxurious bathroom, with large, Jacuzzi tubs and separate showers. Each counter had two sinks and a floor-to-ceiling mirror, and a bidet was located alongside the toilet.

Patty had never seen such elegance.

She chose the bedroom on the right of the sitting room. Patty moved her bags into the bedroom, and, longingly, looked at the king-sized bed.

You know, I'm on vacation. Why not?

Patty flopped into the bed, landing on her back, and promptly fell asleep.

CRENSHAW HAD ESCORTED Brandon back up the hall from his office, and stopped at one of the closed doors. It only opened electronically, and Crenshaw had a key card that he passed through a card reader beside the door. Above the card reader was a panel with four lights. Before Crenshaw scanned the card, a small LED light glowed red. Underneath the card reader, there was a numerical keypad. Crenshaw punched in a five-digit number. On the light panel, another LED light turned orange. A small scanner rolled out of a recess in the wall, and Crenshaw placed his palm on the scanner. It read his palm, and a different LED light lit up. It was yellow. Into a small speaker above the light panel, Crenshaw spoke his name. The last LED light glowed green, and the door lock disengaged.

Brandon nodded once with a slight smile. "Impressive. And very high-tech."

Crenshaw beamed with pride. "It never fails, either. If the power goes out, there are backup batteries sufficient to keep it powered until an electric generator kicks. If you'd like, I can have you and Miss Patty programmed into it, so that you two can check in here from time to time. But only if ya'll want to do it, of course."

"Of course, sir."

Crenshaw pushed the door open, exposing the room inside.

The room was twenty feet wide and forty feet long. Security monitors lined the entire forty-foot long wall across from the entry door. It seemed as if cameras were aimed at every part of the hotel and casino, and, occasionally, scanned part of the camera's viewing area. Some of them would zoom in on individual players, just so that they could make certain no one was trying to cheat. Brandon counted five men that did nothing except watch the monitors. Sometimes they would speak into small microphones that hovered close to their mouths. The microphones were part of a headphone set that worked wirelessly, and had one small speaker in the watcher's ear. The headphone set was held in place with a corresponding piece of plastic that looped over the watcher's head.

The sheer number of monitors would make Dexter Beck, the Justice Security partner who also was their computer geek, drool with lust.

Brandon smiled at this mental image.

A neatly groomed man, dressed in a tailored business suit, stepped over to them. The man was in his mid-thirties, with blond hair and watchful eyes that Brandon guessed didn't miss much. Brandon noticed that the man's shoes were fine Italian leather, and were hand-made at a small shop in Rome. The name of the shop was *Bel Scarpe Abbadelli*, or Abbadelli's Fine Shoes.

Brandon smiled to himself. The only reason he knew about the shoes was because Chris, the man Brandon had just broke up with, had a pair just like them. And they weren't cheap.

Crenshaw said, "Howdy, Mark! I'd like you to meet someone! Mark Brown, this is Brandon King. Brandon's from Justice Security. His partner, Patty Ferguson, is 'freshening up' in their suite."

Brown shook hands with Brandon. "Your reputation...or, rather, your company's reputation...precedes you, Mr. King."

Crenshaw said, "Mark here is my head of security, Brandon."

"Thank you, Mr. Brown. The pleasure is all mine." Brandon gestured around the room. "Very elaborate setup you have."

Brown smiled. "Thanks. As I'm sure you well know, all of it is necessary, both for our own protection in the casino, and for the protection and safety of our guests and employees."

"One thing that Mr. Justice taught me, Mr. Brown, is that all the technology in the world can only be as dependable as the person keeping an eye on it."

Brown smiled with a decidedly superior smirk. "Did he?"

Brandon smiled back. "He did. And I've learned that Mr. Justice knows what he's talking about. Nothing replaces a good, watchful, attentive pair of human eyes in any situation."

Sensing that the two men would soon be arguing over technology versus humans, Crenshaw interrupted. "Now, Mark, none of this electronic crap in here is any damn good if none of you see what it's telling you. Am I right?"

Brown took his eyes off of Brandon to look at his employer. "Yes, Mr. Crenshaw."

To Brandon's ears, it sounded as if Brown agreed with Crenshaw grudgingly...but it also could have been that Brandon took an instant dislike to the man.

Crenshaw responded, "That's right! Now, Mark, take Brandon here and show him everything. If he offers any advice, listen to him, and think about applying it. You good with that?"

Brandon could see that Brown wasn't good with that. The man's mouth might have been closed, but Brandon could see that Brown was clenching his teeth. Hard. He didn't like someone looking over his security empire.

"Sure, Mr. Crenshaw, that would be great."

Brandon, noting some slight sarcasm in Brown's voice, matched it. "Oh, good. I can't wait."

Brown gave Brandon a look that could have melted steel.

NOW, RESTING POOLSIDE with his best friend, Brandon fell asleep.

AT THE JUSTICE SECURITY building, Tony Armstrong was at the front desk. With him was Mark Haase, the night shift desk man, and Emily Owens, Jim Dandy's executive secretary. Tony was going over scheduling with Emily, so that she could oversee the scheduling of the grunts that would be assigned to the new facility.

"Okay, Emily, this work is going to be done by whoever you put in charge as the front desk man at the new building, but, here, a partner has to oversee it all. Here, Misty is in charge of the grunts, and I submit all schedules to her for approval after I've completed them."

"So, will Jim be approving these schedules at the new facility?" asked Emily.

Tony shook his head. "No. At best, there will only be two partners there, and that's only if Joey and the others can convince the extra person to join. They'll be far too busy to take care of this, so it's going to fall to you. Since you're dating Turk, you know that if all partners are out of the building, the executive secretary is in charge. Here, that's Turk. At the new place, it's going to be you. You'll do this as part of your duties there. I don't think it will amount to much, because we won't be using a lot of grunts there. If people start seeing a lot of our uniformed personnel at the new place, they're going to know what the place is. I'm sure word will leak eventually, but it needs to stay secret as long as possible."

Emily nodded. "I agree."

As Tony continued explaining scheduling for uniformed personnel, a four-door sedan double-parked outside on the street. A man got out of the passenger side of the car, and was using two crutches to help him walk. He came toward the double doors, and the car he got out of drove away.

Mark noticed the man. The man had a cast on his lower leg. He was dressed in an off-the-rack suit, and the seam was split on the pants leg so that his suit pants would fit over his cast. The man tucked both crutches under one arm and stood on one leg so that he could pull the door open. He awkwardly entered the lobby, and hobbled toward the reception desk.

Mark tapped Tony on the arm to get his attention. Both men stood and saluted the man in the leg cast. The salute was genuine, because both men had been ex-military, and respected the injury the man in the cast had received. It had happened in the line of duty.

Marcus Moore, the man on the crutches, was embarrassed. This was his first day back at work since the injury. After the arrest of Senator Thompson, Marcus had been instructed to take some time off.

"Will you two please stop that?"

Tony and Mark remained standing. They would remain that way until Marcus returned the salute.

Marcus shook his head. "I've got half a mind to go upstairs and leave you guys standing that way until I leave." He chuckled to himself. To Emily, he said, "Hello, Emily. Good to see you. What should I do about these two knuckleheads?"

Emily smiled at the FBI man. "Salute them back, I guess, Marcus."

Marcus kept a small smile on his face. He stood as straight as possible, and formally returned the salute.

Tony and Mark put their hands down, and immediately held them out to shake hands with Marcus. Marcus shook hands with both.

Tony said, "Marcus, it took a lot of guts to do what you did. I'm proud to know you, sir."

"Hey, Joey and Misty are the two gutsy ones. Misty thought she was dead, and Joey jumped from the plane not knowing whether he could even land safely. And Jim Dandy gets more credit than I do – he caught up to Misty and saved them both."

"Looks to me like there's plenty of credit to go around, Marcus," said Mark.

"Agreed." Marcus looked at the three people. "You look busy. And I didn't think that Mark was on days."

"He is now," replied Tony. "It takes both of us now since we've brought in Jim Dandy's people. We've got more clients, more people coming in and out, and more grunts to assign. I couldn't do it all alone, so the daytime front desk now employs two people."

"Yeah, we're training Emily for the new place, and we've just finished training the new person for nighttime desk duty," added Mark.

Marcus looked at Emily. "The new place is why I'm here. Emily, are you through here? I could sure use some company in Joey's office. You and Jim need to be updated."

Emily looked at Tony. "Can you spare me?"

Tony waved her off. "Sure. Not much more we can teach you anyway."

Emily smiled at Tony. "Good luck with Lena, Tony."

Tony curled his lip at her.

As Emily and Marcus made their way to the elevator, Marcus asked, "I thought that he and Lena didn't hit it off."

Emily laughed. "Lena is the new nighttime desk person. Temporarily, until we move to the new location."

Marcus said, "Oh, crap!" Then he thought about it, and started laughing. "I bet Tony loves that!"

"Tony can't seem to get over the fact that she'll be doing there what he does here. It upsets his equilibrium."

Marcus was still laughing as the elevator doors closed.

AS BRANDON RELAXED by the pool, his mind reflected back to the "tour" that Mark Brown had given him.

As soon as the door had closed behind Crenshaw, Brown had turned to Brandon and said, "Look. I don't want you here, I don't want your advice, and I'm not showing you shit. And you aren't going to say a word to that glad-handing idiot about it, either, or I'll make your time here the worst possible experience of your life. Are we together on this?"

"Back up, Bro...I'm not interested in your job, and I'm not interested in making you look bad. Patty and I are here for a vacation. Period. This stuff that Crenshaw added is news to me." Brandon lowered his voice. "And, if you ever speak to me that way again, I'll kick your ass in front of all these people, and then slice pieces of it off and hand them to you on a platter." Brandon's eyes had turned cold. "Don't think I can't, either. I've been trained by the best, *Mis*-ter Brown." He moved his face close to Brown's. "Whatever your beef is, it's safe to say it isn't with me." He turned to leave the room. "And, if it *is* with me, we can take care of it now. Your choice. As for me, the first recommendation is to hire a head of security that isn't threatened by people that might be able to help out."

Brown's face was beet red. He was angry, but dared not show it.

Brandon left the room, and found his suite. Over dinner that evening, he told Patty all about the meeting with Brown.

"What do you think, Patty? Should I give Big Daddy that recommendation?"

Patty used her fork to move salad around on her plate. Finally, she looked at her friend. "I think we should let it go. Unless he makes trouble. Then, we'll tell Big Daddy everything."

Brandon thought about it. "You're right. I let him know where I stand, so the ball's in his court. I'll let him decide how things go."

Patty smiled. "Good. Let's get adjusted to the place tomorrow, and go swimming day after tomorrow. How's that sound?"

Brandon smiled back. "Great! And I want to hit the casino after swimming. I have a feeling lightning may strike again!"

"Careful that lightning doesn't fry you." Patty forked more salad.

"Ha. Ha." Brandon snapped his fingers. "I know what we need to do tomorrow!"

"What?"

"Let's drive out to the crash site!"

Patty looked at Brandon as if he was crazy. "What for?"

"Just to take a look, of course."

"Brandon. I don't think the FAA has finished their investigation into the crash. I don't think we could even get close."

"Before we left, I overheard Joey telling Louie that the FAA gave the okay to do whatever they wanted to with the wreckage. The plane couldn't be rebuilt." He leaned closer to his friend. "*That* means the crash site is back to what it was before."

Patty still looked skeptical.

"Pleeeease?" asked Brandon.

"All right. Let's go after we swim the day after tomorrow. It isn't that far. Then, we'll come back and hit the casino for a while."

"Deal!"

Now, beside the pool, Brandon couldn't wait to go see the desert and the crash site. When they came the last time, they saw the inside of the hospital and the inside of their hotel. They also saw the inside of the airport. There hadn't been time to sightsee, and it hadn't been the right time, either.

"So, are you through trying to splash me?" asked Patty, keeping her eyes closed.

Brandon, with his own eyes closed, replied, "I guess so. For today, anyway."

"Then let's get this crash site thing over with."

"Okay. Thank you, Patty."

"You're welcome. But it'll cost you."

"Oh, God, what?"

"You have to watch a movie with me."

"God, you're hard to please, Patricia."

"I know."

TURK WENDELL WAS SHAKING hands with Marcus. Turk's huge hand seemed to swallow Marcus's hand.

"Good to see you back, man," said Turk, with his deep voice.

"Thank you, Turk."

Turk winked at Emily, who blushed.

One of the least-kept secrets of the past several weeks was the romance between Turk Wendell and Emily Owens. They had met over the course of an information exchange back when Jim Dandy Security was their competitor. The huge man and the dainty woman had chemistry between them, and they started dating. Both Jim Dandy and Joey Justice knew about the romance, and did not mind one bit. It was actually one of the things that had brought Jim and Joey's friendship back around, although neither one would admit it.

With Emily's forthcoming move to the new building, taking the same position that Turk occupied, she and Turk were facing a long-distance relationship. But both of them were willing to trust that they could make it work out.

"They waitin' for you in Joey's office," said Turk.

"Thanks."

Marcus hobbled over to Joey's office door and knocked.

Joey's voice was clear. "Come in!"

Marcus entered the office to find all seven partner of Justice Security inside. They all burst into applause, with the exception of Jessica. She found it hard to clap with only one hand, but she was slapping her pants leg loudly.

Marcus was surprised by the applause, and then he blushed brightly. Shaking his head, he made his way inside, and closed the door behind him. When he turned back to face his friends, he said, "Smartasses."

"Hey, man, the only smartasses in here are Dexter and Megan," said Louie. "Dey the only ones in here that didn't fall down several thousand feet!"

They all laughed at that.

Joey came over to Marcus and shook his hand. "Glad to have you back on the job, old buddy."

Marcus smiled and replied, "Glad to be back. Now, if this damn leg would heal, I could start giving you all a run for your money."

The rest of the Justice Security partners lined up to shake hands with their FBI liaison.

When they were done, Marcus plopped back into an easy chair. "Okay, I just wanted to update you on your other FBI liaison."

Joey smiled. "How's Tory making it through Quantico?"

Tory Masterson had been a Chicago narcotics cop. During the Chicago mission, he had proven himself good enough to join the FBI. Marcus had offered Tory a position working for him in the city office, but Joey had made a suggestion that Marcus had liked.

"He's almost finished. Once he's done, he'll come here to the city for a little on-the-job training. After that...well..."

Joey looked concerned. "Did you talk to him about what I suggested?"

Marcus nodded. "I did."

The room got very quiet when Marcus didn't continue.

Jim broke the silence. "Okay, I'll ask. Did he go for it?"

Marcus looked at Jim, and then looked at Joey. He deliberately built up the suspense, until even he couldn't stand it. He grinned and said, "He's all for it, and so is his wife. They both want to go be the liaison for the new facility. They're excited that they don't have to raise their kid in a city. That appeals to them as parents. So, Tory's with you, Jim."

Jim pumped his fist in the air. "*Yeah!*"

"I WON'T HEAR ANOTHER word about it! Big Daddy has spoken, and you two will do what I say, and take the damn jeep!"

Crenshaw was speaking to Patty and Brandon.

"I understand how important it is for you two to see that crash site, and the least I can do is give you a ride out there. So, you can use the hotel jeep. Just be sure to take plenty of water with you. And, I want to set you both up with the highest security clearance at the casino. I want you to have the freedom to go where you need to go and do what you need to do."

Brandon shared an anxious look with Patty, and said, "Sir, I don't think your head of security would allow that. He resents us being here, and has bluntly said for us to mind our own business."

Crenshaw smiled. It actually was a very cold smile. Patty was a bit disturbed by it. "You know what? This is my hotel, and I'll do as I please with who I please. Mark Brown doesn't dictate to Big Daddy!" He leaned close to the two young security people. "To tell the truth, he's right to worry. If ya'll work out, Justice Security is gonna be doin' all of my security work, and very soon." He stood straight again. "So, come on! I'll get you set up with clearance...and ol' Mark Brown won't be able to do squat about it!" Crenshaw snickered and snorted at his private joke, as he walked Patty and Brandon through Crenshaw's own highest levels of security.

AN HOUR LATER, THE two young friends drove away in the hotel jeep. They had three bottles of water between them, for what they expected to be a three hour long trip.

Chapter 3

An hour's drive across the Mojave Desert, Patty and Brandon pulled up at the crash site. Patty was driving, and she shut off the engine. They had left the jeep's top and doors at the hotel, so that they could enjoy the sunshine.

Both of them stood up inside the open-topped jeep, and stared over the windshield at the site where Captain Gena Trotter brought the shot-down Justice Security private jet down in an emergency landing.

Most of the plane had been taken away, but there were still small pieces of metal, glass, and plastic strewn around the area. They could see the spot where the nose of the plane impacted, and they looked back at the long rut that the belly of the plane had cut into the floor of the desert. They could see the rock that had snapped off one of the wings of the plane. The wind was blowing toward them from the direction that the plane had come down, and it carried the strong, noxious odor of the dumped jet fuel.

Patty said, "I hope somebody comes along and cleans that fuel up. It looks rough enough out here without that fuel adding to the difficulty of anything's survival."

Brandon said, "I hear you." He took a deep breath. "Maybe if we pass it along to Joey, he'll make sure something is done."

Patty nodded. "Maybe so." She abruptly jumped out of the jeep.

A small bullet hole appeared in the windshield, approximately at the spot that her chest had been. The sound of the shot came a tiny bit later.

Brandon didn't wait. He dove to the passenger side of the vehicle, and began looking for some indication where the shot had come from.

"You okay, Brandon?" asked Patty.

"I'm good. You?"

"I'm good. Where the hell did that shot come from?"

"Not sure. From the looks of the windshield, either front or back."

"My thinking too. You know we're visible on the sides of this jeep, don't you?"

"Rocks?"

"Bet your ass!"

"Okay, Patty, three...two...*one*!"

They ran for the rocks. As they ran, little puffs of sand popped up at their heels, and the sound of shots came to them. When they reached the rocks that the plane had recently accordioned into, they dove for cover. One last shot ricocheted with a vicious whine.

Breathing heavily, Brandon turned to Patty.

"Okay, Blondie, who did you piss off?"

"Me? Who says it wasn't you? You're the one that got into a pissing contest with the head of the hotel's security!"

Another shot rang out, but the bullet came nowhere near them. One of the jeep's rear tires suddenly deflated with a loud "Pwoomp"!

"Oh, no. Brandon, they're shooting the jeep!"

A second shot hit the other rear tire, and, suddenly, the two security agents found themselves stranded in the Mojave Desert, an hour's drive away from the nearest civilization...and who knew how long walking would take.

MARK WAS AT LUNCH, and Tony was at the front desk. He was alone at the moment, because the two men covered each other for breaks.

He glanced outside, and noticed a long, black limousine glide to a stop at the curb in front of the double entry doors. Both front doors opened. On the street side, the driver stepped out, with a dark suit and a cap signifying that he was the driver of a rented limo. The sidewalk side opened, and a middle-aged woman wearing a charcoal pant suit, with moderately high-heeled shoes and a dark blue shirt, stepped out. She wore glasses, had lines of gray through her blond hair, and appeared to be in her mid-forties. She was talking rapidly into a cell phone.

The driver stepped quickly around to the passenger side of the limousine, and opened the door.

Tony grinned from ear-to-ear at the sight of the first person to step out of the back. He turned to his inter-office phone, and called Joey Justice.

"This is Joey."

"Boss, you might want to come down here. And bring everyone with you."

"Why, Tony? What's wrong?"

"Nothing. The prodigal son has come home."

At first, Joey said nothing. Then he broke the silence as he realized who Tony was talking about. "Did he bring *her*, too?"

Tony looked back outside, and the "her" in question stepped out of the limo, and laughingly linked her arm through the man's arm. It looked romantic, until it became obvious that he was supporting her.

"Yes, sir, looks like they're both here."

"Oh, shit." Joey didn't sound happy. "Tony, keep them in the lobby until we get down there!"

"Yes, sir."

"And have Caleb Mitchell meet us there!"

"Yes, sir."

"JESS, ALL I'M SAYIN'" is that I don't think it's fair."

Percival "King Louie" Washington was sitting across from Jessica Queen. Jessica had actually decided to visit Louie in his seldom-used office.

Louie's office was sparsely decorated, and readily demonstrated that he didn't use it much. Louie's assigned clients tended to be sports figures, or people in trouble that required a street-smart security man, and Louie was the go-to guy for those cases. The furniture was utilitarian, and limited to a desk and chair, a couple of bookcases, and three client chairs. The walls displayed a few autographed photos of some of the sports people that Louie had been associated with through one case or another, but also displayed was one of Louie's passions: original art.

Louie was the proud owner of several fine paintings, and had hung only a few in his office. The majority of his prized artwork remained upstairs in his apartment, or in storage at his mother's home in Alabama. He leaned toward fantasy art, and was the proud owner of two original Frank Frazetta paintings. One adorned the wall in his office, and had been used as the cover of and old horror comic, *Creepy*. The other painting was in storage in Alabama, because Louie enjoyed Frazetta's art very much, and felt that he had to keep one painting well away from the violence of his work. He also had paintings on his office walls done by Boris Vallejo and Julie Bell, and a framed print of da Vinci's Vitruvian Man.

"What's not fair, Louie?" asked Jessica. She was seated in one of the client chairs, with her feet up in the other.

"I was countin' on havin' Brandon work with me for a while before he got moved somewhere else. He's *good*, Jess, and I could sure use him. I been shorthanded in my people since Turk got promoted."

"I understand. Have you looked at any of Jim's people? A lot of other good people were folded into our company when he joined us."

"Actually, no, I haven't. I haven't even thought about them."

"It might be worth taking a look at. You might find someone just as good. And talk to Jim – he might be able to recommend someone."

A knock came, and Louie's office door opened. Joey poked his head in.

"Sorry to interrupt, guys, but we have to get to the lobby right now. Especially you, Jessica."

Louie and Jessica both stood.

"What's up, Joe?" asked Louie.

Joey snorted. "Charlie's home, and he's brought his new wife with him."

"And why the bleeding hell do I want to see that drunken harlot?" said Jessica.

"Jessica, please be nice to her. And to Charlie. Carly gives us lots of money, and Charlie keeps convincing her to do it. We have to try to help them." Joey sighed. "Like it or not, Carly's a member of the Justice Security family now. We have to help them if we can."

"I'll be nice to that sodding trollop, but I bloody well won't like it!" said Jessica.

Louie snickered, and Jessica whirled on him.

"And just what's so bleeding funny?"

Louie burst out laughing. "I love it when you get mad. Your Australia comes out."

Joey couldn't help it. He started laughing, too.

Jessica, angry, looked at both men, and said, "*Ohhh...sod off, both of you!*"

Joey and Louie's laughter followed Jessica down the fourth floor hall as she stormed out of the office.

Turk, from his vantage point at the desk across from the elevators, watched Jessica as she stormed into view. He watched her as she stabbed the "down" button with her forefinger several times, apparently with anger. He could hear Louie and Joey laughing as they came down the hall.

Suddenly, Jessica whirled on Turk. "And don't even *think* about laughing, or I'll break this cast over your bloody head!"

Turk just stared back at Jessica with no change of expression. He continued staring as the three partners entered the elevator, and then shook his head in disbelief.

"Woman done gone crazy," he muttered to himself, as he checked housing prices surrounding the new building's location.

"IT'S BEEN THIRTY MINUTES. I think whoever shot at us is gone." Brandon sounded hopeful as he made this observation.

Patty replied with sarcasm. "Wanna step out there and see?"

Brandon was silent for a couple of minutes.

"Patty, if they had wanted to kill us outright, they wouldn't have been peppering our footsteps. Whoever was shooting was a pretty damn good shot." He watched a desert iguana peek out from a small hole in the rocks above him. "I think they're gone. And, besides, I'm thirsty."

"Brandon King, have you forgotten your Louis L'Amour? In the desert, the first person to move sometimes is the first to die! You have to have patience!"

"Patience, schmatience. I'm thirsty."

Brandon abruptly stood up.

No shot was fired.

After a few beats, Patty stood, too.

Still no shot.

They stepped out from behind the rocks.

No shot.

"Okay, maybe you're right. They must be gone."

"Patty, think about it. Why would they stay? They think they've killed us already by shooting out both back tires! They don't know that we have water, or that we've done desert training with Tony and Dexter."

"Brandon, those were simulations. Not the real thing."

"But the training is still better than nothing. We'll be fine, girly. Trust your old friend." He put an arm over her shoulders and hugged. "We've been through worse. Remember when Vincent Lambosa came into the *Kwikstuff* store? That was worse than being out here. I was seriously afraid that I wouldn't get to him before he shot you."

"But you did."

"Only because you trusted me to. This is no different. Trust me. We'll make it."

They walked over to the jeep to gather what little gear they had brought.

One of the three bottles of water had been open, because Patty had just taken a sip.

The bottle was now lying on its side, and its contents were spilled all over the floor of the jeep.

Brandon paled a little. "Okay, I'll give you this one. *Maybe* we'll make it."

Patty turned her head and gave him a frightened look.

"Hey, it's still better than staring at Lambosa's gun between your eyes, or being shot by Fernandez in Chicago, right?"

Patty didn't say anything. She wished she could share her friend's optimism.

WHEN JOEY, LOUIE, AND Jessica got to the lobby, they were the last of the partners to arrive. Carly and Charlie Li were surrounded by Dexter, Megan, Jim, and Misty. Misty had just finished hugging Charlie, and shaking the hand of his new wife.

Jessica was a terrific actress. There was no sign of her intense dislike of the the popular actress as she crossed the lobby, with her arms spread wide to embrace Carly.

"Carly! It's so good to see you again!" said Jessica, as she hugged the not-very-sober actress.

Carly half-heartedly hugged Jessica back. When they stepped apart, Carly asked, "Who are you again?"

Jessica's smile faltered slightly, but came back. "I'm Jessica! Remember? I was taking care of you until Charlie came out and met you in November."

Carly squinted at Jessica. "Oh, yeah, I remember you. You're the bitchy one, right?"

Jessica turned beet red, and was on the verge of exploding.

"Carly, we talked about being polite, remember?" cautioned Charlie. "Jessica is being polite, and is glad to see you. You should be glad to see her, too. She's the reason we met and got married."

"Yeah, whatever. I need a drink, Charlie." Carly's words were slurred.

"Honey, don't you think you've had enough for a while?"

"Then I need to do a line. Or a bowl. Something, okay? Please?"

Charlie smiled nervously at his bosses. "Not right now, honey, okay?"

"Boss?" Tony had waited until there was an opening before he spoke.

"Yes, Tony?" replied Joey.

"Caleb said that he was with a patient, but he would be done in just a couple of minutes."

Inwardly, Joey sighed with relief. Outwardly, he said, "Thank you, Tony. That's good to know."

Misty asked, "Carly, is Charlie keeping you safe and sound?"

Carly giggled. "He is...safe as can be!" She burped a small burp. "Oh, God. Charlie, where's the bathroom?"

Charlie's eyes widened. "Oh, crap! Come on, Carly! This way!"

Charlie took his wife's hand, and hustled the actress to the lobby bathroom.

Dexter said, "Ten bucks says she doesn't make it to the stall."

Tony replied, "I'll take that bet, Dexter. Looks to me like she's well-equipped to hold her liquor."

The couple at least made it to the inside of the men's room.

Caleb Mitchell, the staff psychiatrist at Justice Security, chose that moment to approach the group.

"Hi, Caleb," said Joey.

"Hi, guys," replied the doctor. "I thought Charlie was here with his wife."

Louie made everyone laugh when he said, "She's bowin' down to the porcelain god right now, man."

"She's pretty bad, Caleb," said Joey. "She needs about three months in hard rehab to dry her out and clean her out."

Dr. Mitchell took a deep breath. "Well, in our state, the laws are friendly about that. Charlie can force her into rehab, with a judge's approval, on the grounds that she isn't able to make good life choices herself."

"Do you have to sign off on it, too?" asked Joey.

Caleb nodded.

"Okay, I can find a trustworthy judge, if you want to examine her. Meanwhile, Jessica, while Carly's in with Caleb, would you talk to Charlie, and make sure that this is what he wants to do?"

Jessica nodded. "I can do that. Poor Charlie."

Joey nodded. "Sounds like a plan to me. Let's get it together."

TO PATTY, IT FELT AS if they had walked for miles.

She turned back to look at the jeep, and they hadn't gone very far at all. Maybe half a mile or so.

Crap.

She snuck a look at Brandon. He was walking cheerfully, with his eyes forward, and his head held high.

Well, why not?

The girl that had stared down a gun barrel, and been shot in the shoulder by Esteban Fernandez during the Chicago mission, held her head high, too.

We've definitely been through worse. It's bad when Brandon has to remind me of that. Time to focus on who stranded us out here, and what I'm going to do them once I catch them.

As if he had read her mind, Brandon said, "Wonder who did this to us? Really?"

"I don't know. One thing's for sure, though...whoever it was doesn't have a clue who they're screwing with."

Brandon snorted. "You got *that* right!"

They plodded on for another ten minutes.

"My shoe is full of sand," commented Patty.

Brandon glanced at her feet. "Yeah, Sketchers probably aren't recommended desert footwear."

Patty glanced at Brandon's Nikes. "Oh, and those are *so* much better!"

Brandon smiled and shook his head. "I never said they were better. But they *is* so *fine*!"

Patty laughed at him. "First order of business when we get back to town is for both of us to buy some boots."

"Agreed."

Patty glanced back at the jeep. "Brandon, how could we have walked ten minutes, and the jeep still be the same distance away?"

Brandon laughed. "It isn't, really. Out here, in the heat, distances can be very deceiving. We're probably a couple of miles away from the jeep by now."

Patty's amazement was obvious on her face. "You've got to be kidding."

"I only wish I were."

Fifteen more minutes passed, and both of them were silent, concentrating on taking one step after another.

Brandon broke the silence. He was pointing off to the left. "What's that?"

Patty looked in the direction he was pointing. "I can't tell for sure. Looks like animals of some kind."

Brandon squinted. "I'll be damned. I think you're right!" He glanced at her. "Let's head toward them."

Patty gave him a look. "You *know* animals and I don't get along, Brandon."

"Yeah. But maybe you'll get along with these. At the very least, maybe there's water there."

Patty sighed. "Okay, but I'm telling you this won't end well."

"Yeah, you're right. They're probably running a brothel."

Patty smacked his arm.

CHARLIE LED CARLY BACK to the group in the lobby. His demeanor seemed almost apologetic.

"Carly feels much better now," he told the group.

Caleb stepped forward, and shook hands with Charlie. "Good to see you, Charlie. I don't believe I've had the pleasure of meeting your new wife." Caleb held his hand out to Carly.

"Oh, I'm sorry, Caleb! Caleb Mitchell, this is Carly Stewart. Carly, Caleb is the resident psy..."

Caleb interrupted Charlie. "It's a pleasure to meet you, Carly! I'm a big fan!"

"Who the hell are you? And what do you do here?"

Joey spoke up. "He works here, Carly. And I think he'd like to talk to you a little bit, if you'd give him some time. And I need to speak with Charlie, if you would please let Caleb entertain you for a while."

Carly rolled her eyes, which caused her to stagger a little. Both Charlie and Caleb caught an arm.

"I suppose so, if you just *have* to take Charlie," said the actress.

"Oh, it won't take us long, Carly, and I'd really enjoy your company," said Caleb.

Carly wiggled a finger. "Oh-kay, but no funny stuff. I'm a married woman now."

"No funny stuff. I promise." Caleb led her toward Medical, and his private office.

Tony asked Charlie, "Do I need to get Janitorial into the bathroom?"

Charlie shook his head. "No, she made it to the toilet."

Tony held out his hand, and Dexter put a ten into it, shaking his head.

"Tony, you have the damnedest luck with bets!" said Dexter.

Tony smiled a broad smile.

"Charlie, would you like to talk in the cafeteria over coffee, or up in the situation room?" asked Joey

"Coffee. Please. I need it."

"Then, coffee it is. Tony, please let Caleb know that we're in the cafeteria."

"Will do, Boss."

The group walked toward the cafeteria.

"CARLY, PLEASE SIT DOWN anywhere you'd like." Caleb indicated the chairs, or the couch.

Carly chose the couch. She kicked off her shoes, and tucked her bare feet under her knees, Indian-style.

"So, you know that Charlie is one of our best people. We're all very proud that you two have married."

"Charlie's wonderful."

Caleb looked at her. "Is he?"

The actress nodded. "He is."

"Can you tell me what makes him so wonderful?"

Carly leaned her head on the back of the couch and closed her eyes. "He takes care of me."

"How does he take care of you?"

She looked up at Caleb, focusing for just a moment. "What are you, a shrink?"

Caleb smiled. "As a matter of fact, I am."

Carly laughed. "Of course you are. Charlie wants me to dry out, and he's using you to try to talk me into it."

"He loves you very much, Carly. He worries about you."

She pointed at Caleb, and closed one eye in a long wink. "And *that's* why I love him so much." She put her head back onto the couch. "He worries about me. Nobody else worries about me. On the set, it's always, 'Don't screw this up, Carly' or 'Let's do it right this time, Carly'. It's never 'You feeling okay today, Carly?' or 'What's going on with your life right now?' All they care about is the shoot, or how much skin I'm showing in the scene, or what the damned gossip pages are saying about me." She smiled. "But, Charlie...Charlie worries about *me*. He always wants my opinion. He makes sure that I eat. He always wants me to talk to him...he wants me to share everything with him."

Caleb saw a tear begin at the side of her eye, and roll down her jawline to her neck.

"Nobody's ever cared about just me before." She raised her head to look into Caleb's eyes. Caleb could see the fire there, even through the redness and the lack of focus. "I'd do anything for that man. I'd even give up my career, if he asked me to. Because he loves *me*, and not some image on a screen. He loves my wrinkles, my faults, and my bad bed-hair. When a man holds your head while you're throwing up sour booze into a toilet, that man is worth doing anything for...because he loves you." She swung her legs out from beneath her knees, and planted her feet on the floor. "So, Dr. Mitchell, I know he brought me here to force me into rehab. But I'm going to show Charlie Li how much I love him. I volunteer to go wherever is best. Now. Please set it up, before I fuck up my marriage any more than I already have." She wiped tears from her eyes. "You see, it's all I have, really...the only thing that's real in my life. And I'm not strong enough to quit the booze and the drugs alone. Please help me."

"THEY'RE CATTLE." BRANDON spoke almost with disgust.

Patty looked at them. "Longhorn cattle. They look pretty healthy to me."

Brandon eyed them. "Yeah, they do. But I sure don't want to be on the receiving end of one of those horns."

Patty laughed. "Me, either. But, you're the one that wanted to get closer to them, so here we are."

"Might as well head off in the direction we were going." Brandon turned. "I was actually hoping that there might be a horse mixed in with them, or even a cowboy or two."

"Oh, man, you're kidding, right?" Patty laughed. "What, were you hoping that for a Brokeback encounter?"

Brandon might have reddened a little, but the sun was so bright, Patty couldn't tell. "Maybe," he said, with a slight challenge in his voice.

One of the longhorns, a cow with gray and white fur, turned toward them. She was watching the two of them as they plodded past.

"Brandon, I don't believe you! Even out here, with us fighting for our lives in the desert, and you're thinking about *guys*!"

The cow began walking toward them.

"I'm surprised *you* aren't," retorted Brandon.

The two young people had stopped walking, and were facing each other.

"And how do you know I'm not?"

The cow had gotten within five feet of the two. It stopped walking.

"Because you haven't been talking about anybody. You usually can't wait to tell me all about some new guy that you've got your eye on."

"Well, sor-*ry*! I didn't know that I had to notify you about every cute guy I see!"

"Mooo-*oooo!*" lowed the cow.

Both of the security people jumped and whirled around to see the cow just a few feet away.

"What the *hell*?" exclaimed P atty. She ducked behind Brandon, and peeked over his left shoulder.

The cow didn't flinch.

"Look at this, Patty," said Brandon, with wonder in his voice. "She's not afraid of us. Not in the least."

Patty stepped out from behind Brandon. "Nice cow. Now shoo."

The cow took another step forward.

"Try to pet her, Patty."

"Seriously?"

"Sure! What can it hurt?"

She looked at Brandon. "You *see* those horns, right?"

The cow was looking at Patty.

"Patty, she likes you. Try petting her."

Shaking her head, Patty reached her hand out to the cow's head, which was shoulder-height on the young woman.

The cow lifted her nose, and nuzzled Patty's hand. She took another step toward Patty, and tilted her head under Patty's hand.

Patty began scratching behind the cow's ear. The cow closed her eyes with pleasure.

"Wow," said Brandon. "She's somebody's pet for sure!"

The cow began rubbing the side of her head against Patty. Patty began giggling. "Well, if she's somebody's pet, what's she doing out here?"

Brandon shook his head. "No idea." He reached out to pet the animal.

The cow shied away from Brandon's hand. Brandon pulled his hand back.

"Well, I guess she's a one-woman cow," he said.

"Must be." Patty scratched the cow's ears, and rubbed the animal's head between the two big, soulful, brown eyes.

"Ready?" asked Brandon.

Patty patted the animal on the neck, and said, "Yeah, I guess so."

They started walking again, and the big animal followed docilely behind them.

Chapter 4

Charlie Li sat on the couch in Caleb Mitchell's private office, almost in the same spot that Carly had occupied. Joey sat in one of the chairs, after Charlie had asked him to join them.

"She *volunteered*?" asked Charlie.

Caleb nodded. "Do you want to know why?"

Charlie was still trying to wrap his mind around the idea that Carly had volunteered to go to rehab. But he nodded.

"She loves you, Charlie. She loves you very much. She's doing it so you won't have to worry about her, and so that she can return some of the care you've given her. She said she'd be willing to give up her career if it means keeping you."

Joey saw the tears suddenly well up in Charlie's eyes. In order to give the man a minute, he began talking to Caleb.

"Did she sign papers yet, Caleb?"

Caleb nodded. "She did. We've decided on the inpatient treatment at the Betty Ford Clinic, as you specified."

"Rancho Mirage?"

"I think that would be the best place, yes. I have a friend that works there. She recommends it highly."

"Good enough." Joey turned to Charlie, who had wiped his eyes. "Charlie, a lot of the cost will be covered by the company insurance. If you guys don't think you can cover the rest, let me know, and Justice Security will cover it."

Charlie sniffed. "Sir, I think Carly and I can take care of what isn't covered."

Joey pointed at Charlie. "You let me know if you can't. It's family, so it isn't a problem. Don't let pride get you into a financial bind. That's an order."

Charlie smiled lightly. He was obviously relieved. "Yes, sir."

Joey slapped his knees with his hands. "Okay, that's settled. Now, what are we going to do about the paparazzi?"

Charlie's eyes widened. "Oh, shit...they know we're here?"

"Tony says they're camped outside right now."

Caleb chuckled. "I bet Tony's chomping at the bit over it, too."

Joey smiled. "Let's just say he's not crazy about the idea."

Charlie shook his head. "I'm so sorry, Joey."

Joey smirked. "Not your fault, man. You guys can stay here, in one of the guest suites on the fifth floor." He stood up. "The press won't even know for sure that she's here."

"SO, CARLY, WHAT'S YOUR latest movie about?" asked Misty.

Carly giggled. "I really don't know." She had sobered up a little bit, which made her remark a bit sad. "I honestly just show up, hit my marks, say my lines, and go home to Charlie." Tears came to her eyes. "As funny as it sounds, Charlie makes home for me."

Misty reached over and squeezed the young actress's hand. "I know exactly what you mean."

Carly glanced up at Misty. "Do you?"

Misty nodded.

Carly looked down at her lap. "I just wish I was strong enough to dry myself out. I'm sorry that I'm causing so much trouble."

Misty smiled a gentle smile. "There's no shame in needing help from time to time. We all do."

The two women were seated inside the cafeteria, at a table all to themselves. Some of the personnel on duty...or off-duty, since the cafeteria fed all Justice employees at no cost...would nod to Misty and smile at Carly...and then, they would do a double-take to see if it really was Carly. Both women found it slightly humorous.

"I take it that you don't have famous clients here very often," said Carly.

"Not often, no. But it has happened."

"Wasn't there a model here at one point?"

Misty's mouth became a grim line. "There was, and she turned out to be something else. She killed several of our people here, and Jessica stopped her. With help from Louie and Dexter." She sighed, remembering that night. "It was a close thing."

Carly put her cup of coffee on the table. "Oh, God, I want a drink!" Her hands were shaking, and her face was pale.

Misty smiled. "Come with me. I'll take you to someone that might be able to help you with that."

BRANDON SQUINTED AT the sun. "It's going to set in a few hours, and we've still got who knows how many more miles to go. I don't think we're going to make it back tonight."

The cow was still plodding along behind them, following Patty. The animal showed no signs of being tired, or being exceptionally thirsty. It had adapted itself to living in the desert.

Patty glanced back at the animal. "Brandon, I'm getting an idea."

"I'm all ears, since we're down to one full bottle of water."

"Stand here, and let me try something."

Brandon stood still, watching his friend.

Patty walked slowly toward the longhorn cow, not really believing that she was really going to trust an animal, given her not-so-glorious past with the great outdoors. But, she walked over with her hand out, speaking in a baby-talk tone to the large creature.

Patty moved behind the horns, patting the cow down on its neck, sides, and back. The animal moved its head with pleasure at the attention, and Patty took her time to pet the animal all over those areas. She then hugged the animal's neck, squeezing fairly tightly. The animal enjoyed this. Patty then laid her upper body over the cow's back, and rested her head against the animal.

The animal didn't move, and seemed to have no surprise at the human's peculiar actions.

"Brandon, can you come over here?"

He walked over to stand beside Patty. "I'm here."

Patty was still draped over the cow's back. "Boost me up."

Brandon's eyes widened. "Patty, you can't be serious! This thing only outweighs us by about a thousand pounds or so!"

"I'm serious. This animal was someone's pet, and I'm willing to bet that it's been ridden before. So, boost me up."

"Patty, that may be a losing bet! This animal could easily kill both of us!"

Patty raised herself up to look at Brandon. "This from the man that told me to trust the occasional gamble?"

Brandon thought for a minute. "Okay, I'll do it. But I still think it's too big of a gamble."

Patty thought so herself, but she wasn't going to admit it to Brandon. "Come on, boost me up before I lose my nerve."

Brandon made a stirrup with his hands, and stooped. Patty put one foot into Brandon's hands, and stepped up onto the longhorn's back.

The cow didn't move.

"I don't friggin' believe it," muttered Brandon.

Patty leaned forward, and stretched out so that she was lying on the cow's neck with her upper body. Her head was beside its ears. "Giddyup, girl," she said, as she pressed the cow's sides with her heels.

The cow began to walk, carrying Patty with her.

"I don't friggin' believe it," muttered Brandon again.

Patty put one hand on each horn. She pulled on the cow's horn with her left hand, and the cow turned left. Encouraged, she pulled on the cow's horn with her right hand, and the cow turned to the right. She pulled with both hands, and said, "Whoa, girl." The cow stopped.

Patty looked back at Brandon and held out her hand to boost him up. "Come on, cowboy, we got us a ride!"

"CLOSE YOUR EYES. CONCENTRATE on what is deep inside you. Find your center."

Dexter Beck sat on a small mat across from Carly Stewart in a small room inside the company's gym. Carly also sat on a mat. Both had their legs crossed underneath them, and their hands rested on their knees, palms up.

"Listen to my voice, Carly. Focus on your inner healing powers. You are in charge of your body. You can make yourself relax."

Carly was breathing steadily.

Dexter continued speaking to her in quiet, confident tones. Finally, he felt that she was ready.

"Carly, I want you to listen to my voice, and only my voice. I want you to concentrate on relaxing. Just relax. Are you relaxed?"

"Mmm-hmm."

"I want you to picture yourself sitting in a field of daisies. Just daisies, as far as the eye can see. They're swaying in the breeze, bobbing their flowered heads in rhythm with each of your breaths. Can you see the daisies, Carly?"

This time, when she murmured "Mmm-hmm", it was so faint that Dexter could barely hear it.

"Somewhere in this field of daisies is a sunflower. Carly, that sunflower is your ability to heal yourself. Can you see the sunflower, Carly?"

Carly's brow wrinkled, as if she were staring off into the distance. "Uh-uh." Again, a quiet murmur.

"Look all around you, Carly. The sunflower is actually very close to you. You should be able to see it."

"I see it." So quiet.

"That sunflower is always there, Carly. It's always inside you. It's your center, and it will help you heal yourself. Do you understand?"

"Mmm-hmm."

"When you feel lost, or if it seems too much for you to take, you can close your eyes and find that sunflower again. Your strength comes from it, because its roots are in your heart."

Carly smiled a tiny smile.

"Now, look around the field again, Carly. Do you see a large, red rose? It might even be bigger than the sunflower. Look all around you. Do you see it?"

Carly smiled. "Mmm-hmm."

"Carly, that rose is so big. It's much bigger than your sunflower. It's comforting, isn't it?"

"Mmm-hmm."

"That rose is Charlie's love for you. If your sunflower ever needs extra power, that rose will give it whatever it needs. Because your strength and Charlie's love are really all you need to conquer your problems. Do you see how they intertwine, Carly?"

"Mmm-hmm."

"They're always there. Now, I want you to count backward. Start at ten, and when you get to one, you'll be sound asleep. But while you sleep, your sunflower will be filling you with its strength, Carly. It will keep you from craving poisons for the rest of today. Do you understand?"

"Mmm-hmm."

"And, when you wake, you'll feel the full warmth of Charlie's love and the full strength of your sunflower's power. You'll be in control of the problems facing you. Do you understand, Carly?"

"Mmm-hmm."

"You may start counting now."

Carly began sleepily counting backward. "Ten. Nine. Eight. Sseven. Sixxxx..."

The young actress was now slumped over her lap, fast asleep.

Dexter rose silently, and exited the room.

Misty waited outside the room, leaning against the wall beside Charlie Li.

"She'll sleep for about half an hour. I don't think she'll want any alcohol or drugs today, but she'll forget as time passes. Charlie, you'll need to remind her to find her sunflower from time to time. And ask her counselors at the clinic to do the same."

Charlie held out his hand, and Dexter shook it.

"Dexter, thank you."

Dexter waved Charlie off with a smile. "Don't mention it, man! I'm glad to do it for you! And if you ever need more help, call on me. When's your flight back?"

"Joey's flying us out tomorrow on the private jet."

"Good. At least this one shouldn't get shot down."

Misty smiled at her friend. "Thanks, Dex. Hey, does Caleb know that you can hypnotize people?"

Dexter smiled a mischievous smile. "Nope. And I don't ever plan to tell him." He turned again to Charlie. "Tell her to remember that her strength comes from within, and from the rose. That's all that she'll need to conquer those inner demons. Without that desire from inside her, nobody will ever be able to do anything for her. Remind her of that, will you?"

Charlie nodded. "Will do."

Dexter looked around the gym. "I thought Louie was coming here."

Misty shook her head. "I don't know, Dexter. I haven't seen him since we all left the lobby."

Dexter shrugged. "Oh, well, we'll work out later, I guess. I think I'll go down to the computer lab and see what Megan's working on."

PATTY AND BRANDON WERE a couple of miles outside Carson City, thanks to the longhorn cow.

"You gonna name this cow?" asked Brandon.

Patty nodded. "Yeah. I think I'm gonna name her 'Flame.'"

Brandon thought for a minute, and then nodded. "Good name."

"I'LL BE READY TO DRIVE to the second location tomorrow, Joe," said Jim Dandy.

Jim was sitting in Joey's office with Misty and Emily.

"That's good, Jim. Construction crews should start arriving within a week or so. This should give you time to find housing for all of you."

"Well, it's only me, the kids, and Emily right now."

"I know. But, once the building is livable, that should increase. That's the construction crew's priority – make the apartments livable. Once that's done, everything else will fall into place."

"I'll be coming in a couple of days, Jim. Turk and I still have to work out our personal plans for this," said Emily.

Misty shook her head. "I wish we could spare Turk, Emily. Maybe if we find a replacement..."

Emily smiled. "Misty, Turk and I have already talked it out. We'll do it this way for now."

Joey smiled. "Emily, we'll work something out as soon as we can. A six-hour separation is hard to handle in a relationship."

"Thank you, Joey." Emily turned to Jim. "Jim, if you don't need me right now, I want to go study more procedures with Tony."

Jim smiled. The light glinted off of his white teeth. "Go ahead, Em. I won't need you."

Emily smiled at her boss, and rose to leave the room.

Once the door closed behind her, Joey commented. "Jim, you found a great executive secretary. You know that, right?"

Jim nodded. "I did. Even in the Sullivan building, she knew more about our business than I did."

Misty nodded. "Jessica was that way before she became a partner, and Turk is like that now. Patti never had the chance to get that far."

Jim shook his head. "I remember that night. I wish I had called in some people to help around the arena. Maybe Fernandez wouldn't have gotten to Patti."

"Maybe so, Jim," said Joey. "But we can't keep beating ourselves up over that. Fernandez has done much worse."

The three partners nodded.

FLAME WALKED INTO THE parking lot at Big Daddy's at sunset. Two of the valets were outside, and saw Patty give Brandon a hand down from the big cow's back. Patty stayed on her back, and guided the animal over to the valets.

Both were male, and dressed as cowboys. They began laughing when Patty stopped the animal.

"Lookie there, Bob! It's a real cowgirl!"

"First one I ever saw ridin' a cow, though."

"Yeah, me too. Say, ain't you that Patty girl?"

Patty gave the man a look. "Yes."

"Well. Cowgirl Patty, Bob!"

"How 'bout just plain ol' Cow Patty, Steve?"

Both men burst out laughing.

Patty turned beet red. She turned to Brandon. "Give me your belt."

Brandon took off his belt and handed it to her. She took her own belt off, and looped the two together. Then, she climbed down off of the cow's back, and hooked the belt over Flame's horn in a makeshift lead rope. She tied the cow to one of the posts supporting the hotel's porch roof.

"Please get her some water, would you? And maybe some hay?" She gave the two laughing men a stern look.

"Sure thang, Cow Patty."

Bob turned to Brandon. "I think ol' Mark Brown's lookin' for you, sir."

Brandon's look was blank. "Thanks."

"Don't mention it." He turned back to Patty. "He didn't say nuthin' about you, there, Cow Patty."

Patty punched the man in the stomach as hard as she could. He bowed over from the punch, and had to take several deep breaths before he could breathe again.

"Water and hay for my animal, please."

The valet that was still standing was wide-eyed. "Y-yes, *ma'am!* Right away, ma'am!" He scurried off to find water and hay for Flame.

Patty turned to the longhorn. "You stay right here, girl."

The cow snorted, gazed lovingly at Patty, and looked content.

Chapter 5

"Where have you two been?" hissed Mark Brown. He had taken Brandon by the arm, and was hustling him through the lobby and into the hallway leading to the security room, and to Crenshaw's office.

"What the hell are you doing?" asked Brandon. "You got about two seconds to get your hand off of my arm, Brown!"

"I strongly recommend that you do just that, Mr. Brown," added Patty.

Brown moved his hand. "Sorry. I'm just a little tense right now."

Patty looked at the security head's face. "What's happened, Mr. Brown?"

Brown looked around the hall, and then guided the two young people into the employee lounge. The lounge was deserted.

"What's going on, Brown?" asked Brandon.

Brown took a breath. "I went into Crenshaw's office a few minutes ago. I needed him to sign some money transfer papers. He's dead. Shot. Through the temple."

Brandon and Patty both looked at Brown with surprised expressions.

"Big Daddy's dead?" said Patty.

"Oh, shit," said Brandon.

Brown looked flustered. "I tried to find you two. I...well, I just..." He sighed. "For all my bluster, I've never dealt with anything like that before. I don't know what to do!"

Brandon rolled his eyes. "Have you called the police?"

"I...no. I wasn't sure that I should."

"Are you kidding me?" said Brandon. "We *have* to call the police! We'll get in trouble if we don't!"

"Right. I understand. I'll...I'll just..."

Patty interrupted the man's stammering. "Was the office door locked when you found him?"

"Um...no. No, it was unlocked."

"Did you lock it back?"

Brown nodded.

"Okay, good. That means nothing has been touched. The police will think that's important."

"Right." Brown looked terrified. "Guys, I'm sorry. I never thought I'd have to deal with something like this. I apologize for the way I've treated you two."

Patty waved him off. "Never mind that now, Mr. Brown. Brandon, why don't you call the police, and I'll call home."

"Home?" asked Brown.

Patty nodded. "Yes. Our boss has to know."

MISTY, JIM, AND JOEY were discussing dinner plans. They actually planned to go out to eat, instead of the cafeteria or the kitchen in Joey and Misty's sixth floor apartment.

Turk interrupted their deliberations by poking his head through the office door.

"Boss, you got a phone call."

"Can it wait, Turk?"

The big man shook his head. "Patty. She sound pee-oh'd."

Joey shook his head. "Okay, thanks, Turk." He picked up his desk phone. "Hi, Patty. What's wrong?"

Joey listened to the young woman.

"Hold on, Patty. I'm in my office with Misty and Jim. Let me put you on speaker, and you can repeat what you just said." Joey pressed the button that put the call on speakerphone. "Go ahead, Patty."

"I said, Homer Crenshaw has been shot and killed in his office. Brandon is calling the police right now."

All three partners shared a look.

"Patty, do you know who did it?" asked Misty.

"No, ma'am."

Jim spoke up. "Have you seen the body?"

"No, sir. We were just told about it by the hotel's head of security."

Joey asked, "How long ago was he killed?"

Patty asked the question, and they could hear Brown talking in the background.

"Mr. Brown says he found the body about thirty minutes ago."

"And he waited this long to tell you and Brandon? And to call the police?" Joey was incredulous.

"Yes, sir."

Jim asked, "Patty, why did he wait so long to tell you and Brandon?"

Patty sighed audibly. "We've been stranded in the Mojave, sir. Brandon and I visited the crash site, and someone shot at us. Then, they shot out our jeep's tires. We had to walk a good part of the way back to town."

"This might be important to the police, Patty," said Misty. "Who gave you the ride back to town?"

Patty sighed again. "We rode a cow back to town, ma'am."

Joey and Jim burst out laughing, and Misty smiled a bit.

"A cow, Patty?" asked Misty.

"Yes, ma'am, a longhorn. It likes me, and let us ride. It's outside, being given water and hay right now." Patty decided to level with her bosses. "The valets called me 'Cow Patty'. I punched one of them."

Joey and Jim started laughing even harder. Misty caught herself chuckling a little.

"Patty," said Misty through a smile, "are you two okay? Do you need us?"

"No, ma'am, we'll be all right. We're going to help the police as much as we can, and if they can't figure out who killed Big Daddy, then Brandon and I will."

Jim was calming down from laughing, and asked, "Patty, are you sure? I mean, we're all here to help if you think you need it."

"We'll be fine, sir. Thank you."

Joey said, "You call us if you need us, Patty. That's an order."

"Yes, sir." Patty hesitated. "There is one thing..."

"Name it."

"Mr. Dandy, would you find out if there's someplace that I can board this cow at the new location? I want to give Flame a good home."

Struggling to keep his laughter inside, Jim said, "I will be glad to, Patty."

The partners barely got the phone disconnected before they burst into fresh laughter.

PATTY'S FACE WAS VERY red when she disconnected the call.

"K-I-N-G. That's right. Yes. Yes, he's right here." Brandon covered the mouthpiece on the landline phone in the lounge, and held the receiver out to Mark Brown. "They want to talk to you."

Brown's mouth was a grim line as he took the phone. "This is Mark Brown."

Brandon turned to Patty. "So, how did they take it?"

"Apparently, I'm now the laughingstock of the company, thanks to those two idiots out front. I'm tempted to go punch one of them again."

Brandon let a smile escape before he clamped down firmly on it. "What did they say?"

"Joey said that if we need anything, just let them know."

"That's fine. Yes. I'll meet you at the front door. Yes, they'll be with me. Yes, I agree. I think drawing as little attention to the situation as possible is a good idea. Right. We'll be there." Brown hung up. Without turning, he said, "That was the sheriff himself. He's coming out, with a couple of deputies. He says he'll keep it quiet, but I don't trust him." He turned to Brandon and Patty. "He wants you two there, too."

"Glad to, but why? We haven't even seen the body!" said Brandon.

"He's an asshole, that's why." Brown shook his head. "Mr. Crenshaw told me that if anything ever happened to him, I was to call his lawyer. Hell, that shyster was just here this afternoon! Won't he be surprised that he has to come back?" He picked up the wall phone, and began dialing the number. "The old bastard better be sober, is all I have to say."

JOEY HAD CALLED EACH of the other partners to inform them about the situation with Brandon and Patty.

Word had circulated through the building about it, along with Patty's new nickname. Louie had been the reason that the nickname leaked out, as he had answered his cell phone in the middle of the cafeteria, surrounded by several plainclothes personnel. He had repeated "Cow Patty" before he thought about where he was, and realized what he had said after he said it.

Sheeeiiittt, he thought to himself. *Little girl won't ever forgive me for lettin' that out.*

Jim had said his goodbyes, and had just driven away from the building.

He became lost in thought.

I wonder if they're okay. Surely, they've handled murder cases before. Joey and Misty said that they're the best of the best. That's why they've been promoted not just to plainclothes, but in charge of plainclothes at the new building.

Nah, they'll be fine. Brandon's very smart, and very quick with his reflexes, and Patty's a bulldog when it comes to doing her job. They're fine.

But they're mine. They used to be Joey's, but now they're mine. And they're out there all alone.

And they're so young.

Of course, I was young once. Everyone has to start somewhere.

But they're mine. I want them to know that they can depend on me.

And they're so young.

Grinning at himself and shaking his head at feeling like a mother hen, Jim Dandy abruptly turned his car toward the airport, and booked a flight to Carson City as he drove. He got lucky, and booked the last seat on a flight that was leaving in thirty minutes. He just had time to clear himself through the TSA checkpoints and board the plane.

Can't hurt them to have a little backup.

"BOSS, I HAVEN'T HAD a vacation in three years. I'm asking for two weeks, starting now. Is that okay?"

Tony Armstrong stood in front of Joey's desk, almost standing at attention. His request had caught Joey by surprise.

"Well...sure, Tony, if you want it...Who can cover for you?" stammered Joey.

"Mark will take day shift, and Lena can take nights."

Joey waved his hand as he spoke. "Okay, then, sure, Tony. You're on vacation. Have a good time."

"I will, Boss. Thanks."

Tony turned on his heel, and abruptly marched from the office.

Joey watched the man's back as he walked away.

I just wonder what brought that *on so sudden...*

MISTY WILHITE WAS IN the sixth-floor apartment she shared with Joey. She pressed "send" on her cell phone, hoping that she was doing the right thing.

The other end of the call rang, then rang again. It was then answered.

"Marcus Moore."

"Marcus, this is Misty."

"Hi, good-lookin'! Did you finally decide to ditch Joey for a wild life of government pay?"

Misty smiled. "No, not happening, you crazy man."

"Yep, my luck's still the same," replied Marcus, with a laugh in his voice. "What's wrong?"

"Well, it's about the kids," she said, and then she explained the situation to Marcus. "I'm sure they're fine, and they can handle it all, but I was wondering if you could maybe pull some strings in the Carson City FBI office, and get someone to check on them."

"I can, or some heads will roll. Leave it to me, and don't worry about Patty and Brandon. I got this."

"Thank you, Marcus. Not a word to Joey, now, okay?"

"No problem, lady. You stop worrying. I'll take care of the kids."

THE MAN IN THE COWBOY hat and the sheriff's badge swaggered up to the entry doors at the front of Big Daddy's. Mark Brown was standing just inside the doors, with Patty Ferguson and Brandon King beside him.

Patty had suggested that they stay inside for the sake of the valets. Brown agreed after he caught a glimpse of Brandon nodding vigorously from behind Patty.

The sheriff was about six-one, and obviously thought he was quite good-looking. He almost strutted through the doors as he entered the building. He nodded at Brandon, nodded at Mark Brown and said, "Brown," as an acknowledgement. Then he turned to Patty, touched his hand to his hat brim, and said, "It's a fair pleasure to meet you, ma'am. I'm the sheriff here...name's Bart Josephs."

Patty looked the sheriff up and down, and said, "Uh-huh."

A small hint of anger flashed across the sheriff's face and disappeared just as quickly.

Brown saw this, and actually hid a smile.

Score one for the blond chick, thought Patty.

Two deputies followed the sheriff in. Neither one looked very intelligent, but appearances could be deceiving, as Patty well knew.

Josephs looked around to make sure that the deputies hadn't heard Patty's response. They hadn't, or if they did, they didn't show it.

"So, Brown, where's these two hotshots from Justice Security?"

Brown smiled widely, and aimed a thumb at Brandon. "This is one of them, Sheriff. Brandon King."

Josephs nodded at Brandon, who nodded back.

"The other one is the young lady that just told you that she wasn't interested. Patty Ferguson."

Josephs turned beet red, and glanced sideways at Patty. He mumbled something to her, but all she understood was, "...sorry...meetcha..."

Brown said, "Big Daddy's lawyer is here, too, Sheriff. He's at the front desk, waitin' for you."

Josephs looked toward the front desk. "I'll be damned. Addison Slade. Big Daddy always went for the best, didn't he?" He shook his head. "Well, then, let's go talk to him, and then we'll see the body." Josephs began to walk to the desk, but one of his deputies said something to him, and he stopped. A look of remembrance crossed his face, and he snapped his fingers. "Oh, yeah! Brown, there's a cow outside. You want us to take it over to the slaughterhouse for you?"

"Better ask the lady that the cow belongs to, Sheriff," replied Brown, indicating Patty.

Josephs turned to look at the young woman. "That's *your* cow, ma'am?"

"After today, she sure is."

Brandon noticed two men hovering close by. They seemed to be watching, but trying not to be seen watching. His eyes narrowed.

"Ma'am, you can't have livestock in front of this hotel."

"Who says?"

Josephs stood straight up, extending himself to his full height. "I do."

Patty shook her head. "Sorry, Sheriff, you'll need more than that before Flame goes anywhere."

Josephs looked incredulous. "*Flame?* You've named that mangy, range-worn old piece of walkin' leather *Flame?*" He began laughing. "You gotta be kiddin' me!"

Patty was getting angrier by the minute. Just as she opened her mouth to say something, the two men that had been hovering close by stepped up.

The first one said, "Sheriff Josephs, you're not interfering with a duly deputized Federal officer performing her duty, are you?"

The other man said, "Yeah, we'd hate to have to arrest you in your own jurisdiction, right in front of your deputies. Be a little embarrassing, wouldn't you say?"

Patty, Brandon, and Mark Brown were staring at the two men. None of them knew the two.

But the sheriff did.

"Federal officer? *Her?*"

The first man nodded. "That's right. And so's the young man."

"I'd tread carefully, if I were you, Sheriff," added the second man.

Patty couldn't stand it. "Who are you guys?"

The first man smiled at Patty. "I'm Tomlinson, and he's Hickerson." He took out his badge and ID. "We're FBI, Ms. Ferguson, just helping out where we can."

"We had a call from a big honcho back in your city. He asked us to look out for you two." Hickerson looked at the sheriff. "Knowing this guy, it's a good thing we came out."

"Was this honcho's name Marcus Moore?" asked Patty.

Tomlinson nodded. "Yes, ma'am. That was the man."

Brandon started laughing. "The boss called out the troops, Patty."

At first, Patty felt frustrated. Then, she started thinking about it, and realized something that stunned her.

It was Justice Security's way of letting Brandon and Patty know that the company had their backs.

Patty smiled at that, and joined Brandon in his laughter.

"Just to let you know, Bart," said Tomlinson, "These two have higher Federal clearances than our SAC back at the office."

Hickerson added, "I've heard the words 'he was sent to Guantanamo' alongside the words 'Justice Security.'"

The sheriff's face turned red, and then paled. His deputies were hiding smiles behind their faces. To them, it was nice seeing this man brought down from an attempt to intimidate a seemingly helpless young woman to cringing and trying to hide his fear.

"Ms. Ferguson, Mr. King...we're around if you need us." Tomlinson handed Patty a business card. "That number will reach either of us twenty-four hours a day."

"Thank you, sir," said Patty. She was humbled.

Hickerson turned back to Josephs. "Next time, Bart, you might want to find out who it is you're trying to scare. From what I heard from back east, this girl could kick your ass without breaking a sweat. And the young man could slice you up and fry you for breakfast."

Tomlinson was nodding. He then thrust his face into the sheriff's. "I'd surely pay good money to see that, too."

Hickerson opened a gym bag that he had been holding. He reached inside and took out two Glock semi-automatic pistols, complete with holsters, belts, and two boxes of ammunition each. "Mr. Moore said to make sure that you two were armed, and that I needed to let law enforcement know that you have Federal carry permits wherever you go."

Patty and Brandon each took a weapon.

Patty had never felt so connected...so *belonging* to something in her life.

"THEY CALLED HER WHAT?" asked Megan Beck.

"Cow Patty," answered Dexter Beck.

Megan sat quietly and stewed. "And she *took* it?"

Dexter smiled. "No, honey. She punched the guy, according to Joey."

Megan sat quietly a bit longer. She and Dexter had just finished a late supper. He had told her about the situation in Carson City over the meal. She'd been in the computer lab all day, and hadn't heard.

"And they don't know anything else about the killing?"

Dexter smiled behind his coffee cup. "Not that I've heard."

Megan stood up, and began pacing around their dining room. She was flexing her hands open and closed.

Dexter was still smiling as he observed his wife. He was waiting for her to say something.

"Do you think they'll be okay, Dex?" she asked.

"Probably," he said through his smile.

Megan heard the smile. She turned to him, and came over to him. She sat in his lap, and ran her hand over his head.

"Can we go check on them, honey? Please?"

Dexter started laughing. "Honey, I already booked a charter flight for in the morning. I knew you'd want to go. We take off at four AM."

Megan smiled broadly. "Can we bring some things that make noise? And things that have triggers?"

Dexter nodded once. "If it makes you happy, Rambo."

Megan squealed with delight, and bear hugged her husband. "You are the *best* husband *ever!*"

LOUIE AND JESSICA WERE in the cafeteria. The staff dessert cook had made blueberry cobbler, and it was a favorite of both partners.

"Jess, it ain't right."

Jessica smiled. "What's wrong now, Louie?" Jessica's right arm was the broken one. She was using her left hand to eat her cobbler, and, even after four weeks, was having trouble making it work properly.

"Brandon. Patty. We ought not to leave them out there in Carson City to fend for themselves. We should be backing them up, letting them know that they're part of Justice Security."

Jessica put down her spoon, and picked up her coffee to take a sip. "You don't think they feel part of the company?"

Louie shook his head. "Naw. I know they do." He chuckled to himself. "They just so young, Jess. It's like worrying about younger brothers and sisters. You try to watch out for them."

Jessica put down her cup, and picked up her napkin. "You and I could slip out there. Make a quick trip before anyone knows we're gone." She wiped imaginary coffee from the sides of her mouth. "You know...just to make sure that they're all right."

Louie's face brightened. "Yeah! I'm not really up to speed yet! Dr. Bishop told me to keep out of situations that could give me another concussion." He pointed at Jessica's arm, which she politely held up for him to see. "And your arm won't be healed for another two weeks. We ain't no good for much right now, anyway, so nobody will miss us." He banged the table. Their dishes rattled loudly, and Jessica jumped in her chair. "Let's do it! Let's go, Jess!"

"Do you mind if I finish dropping my cobbler across the front of my blouse first?"

Chapter 6

"All right, Brown, I guess we've dallied around enough in here," said Josephs. "Lead the way to the body.

Brown waved his hand to get the attention of Addison Slade, who was leaning an elbow on the front desk, waiting patiently. When Slade saw Brown's wave, he stood upright, and strode in the group's direction.

Josephs nodded to the attorney. "Slade."

Slade nodded back. "Sheriff."

"The sheriff wants to see the body now, Mr. Slade," said Brown.

"By all means." Slade waved a hand in the direction of the employees' hallway.

Josephs told his two deputies to remain in the lobby.

As the group approached the door to the hallway, Brandon asked the sheriff a question.

"Sheriff, Patty and I have just gotten back into town. We were stranded in the desert today, and we haven't even seen the body. Why exactly did you want us with you?"

"Material witnesses."

Addison Slade gave the sheriff a look with his eyebrows raised. The question was obvious.

"Sheriff, I agree that these two young people need to stay around. I have my own reasons for requesting that they remain, which I will make known shortly. But, if they were in the desert all day, what material did they witness?" Slade's voice was smooth, deep, and inquisitive.

"Okay, how about this, then: I don't like 'em, I don't like the company they work for, and I want them with me just so that I can inconvenience them. It's a murder investigation, and I can inconvenience anybody I like."

Slade smiled, which meant nothing. "That remains to be seen, Sheriff."

They had all stopped in front of Crenshaw's office door.

Brown told the group, "Right after Mr. Slade left, he called me in to tell me that he had added clearance to everything for Mr. King and Ms. Ferguson. After we discussed that, he asked me to fetch last night's casino reports, along with a cash transfer form, and bring them to him. I left, and pulled the door closed behind me. I went into the security room, retrieved the reports, checked a couple of monitors, signed off on a couple of reports, and came back here. I was only gone for about ten minutes. The office door was locked. I knocked, but I didn't hear anything. I thought he had left on some errand, or maybe was in the bathroom, so I unlocked the office. I was going to leave the papers on his desk."

Brown unlocked the office door. "When I opened the door, I saw this." He swung the double doors wide.

The upper half of Homer Crenshaw's body was lying across the big desk. He was hatless, and there was a neat, round hole in his temple. Patty couldn't tell from this distance what caliber it was, but it looked big...like the entry hole of a forty-five. Crenshaw's eyes were open, but they were facing down, eternally staring at the top of the desk, as if he were inspecting minute flaws in the richly polished wood. He had died almost instantly, because there was very little blood on the surface of the desk. His hands were visible, and both were palm-down. One was stretched out a little farther than the other.

Patty felt a small lump of sadness inside at this man's death.

"How far inside the office did you go, Brown?" asked the sheriff.

"I took about three steps inside. I realized he was dead, and I turned around and left the room. I locked the door behind me."

"Why'd you kill him?"

Brown turned his head to Josephs. "I didn't."

"Then why did you look for these two before you called me?" The sheriff aimed a thumb at Patty and Brandon.

"Truthfully?" Brown looked at the two of them. "I'm sorry, but I thought maybe one of them had done it."

"Uh-huh. And what made you change your mind?"

"They were stranded in the desert, just like they said. They came riding into the parking lot on the back of a damn cow."

"'Flame.'"

Patty felt herself turning red again. "Yes. Flame. She's a good cow."

The sheriff snorted.

Slade interrupted. "Was that the cow I saw outside, Ms. Ferguson?"

"Yes, it was. We found her out in the Mojave with several other longhorns. She started following us. She seems to have adopted me, and she let Brandon and I ride her back into town."

Slade smiled. "I know that cow. She used to belong to a young girl – a little younger than you – that died a couple of years ago. She had that cow ever since it was a calf." He shook his head sadly. "Cancer killed that girl. She treated that cow like a most folks would a puppy. She's sleep out in the barn with it, all snuggled up under a big blanket on some clean straw. Her folks went broke trying to keep the medical people paid up. They finally gave up, turned the cows out into the desert, and moved back east somewhere. I lost track." The attorney smiled at Patty. "The girl's name was Hannah Marie Newman. I think she'd be pleased that her cow has taken up with someone that will love that animal."

Patty felt a tingling on her skin, and warmth spread inside her body. "What did Hannah name the cow, Mr. Slade?"

"Doesn't matter, Ms. Ferguson. She's *your* cow now, and if she answers to 'Flame', then 'Flame' is who she is."

"Well, if we're through with all the namby-pamby, honey-drippin' feelgoods now, can we please go back to figurin' out who killed this man?" The sheriff sounded very sarcastic.

"No need to be an ass, Sheriff." Brandon's tone was plain...with a hint of threat.

"You got somethin' to say to me, mister?"

Slade interrupted. "Sheriff, I think I'd be a little more polite to these two young people. They own this place now."

"*What?*"

Brown added his question. "What do you mean, Mr. Slade?"

"That's why Mr. Crenshaw called me out here today. He wanted me to record his last will and testament." He held up a flash drive. "It's all here. He didn't have any family at all. He left everything he had to Brandon King and Patty Ferguson."

Both Brandon and Patty had wide eyes and wider mouths.

"HI, MARCUS. WHAT'S up?" Joey had answered his phone.

"Hey. When are you taking the actress to the clinic?" asked Marcus.

"The four of us – Carly, Misty, Charlie, and I – are all flying out in the company's private jet at six AM sharp."

"Mind if an FBI agent with a broken leg hitches a ride? And gets dropped off in Carson City on the way?"

"Marcus! You hate flying! Especially after what we just went through! Are you worried about the kids?"

"Aren't you?"

Joey was quiet for a few beats, as he thought about it. "Yeah, I guess I am. A little."

"A little?"

"All right, a lot. What about it, G-Man?"

"Why don't we all stop, and check on them? I can make sure that nobody's trying to railroad them, or anything."

"Sure. If our actress can make it without drinking...or doing anything else, I don't see a problem. I've already ordered the pilots to remove all alcoholic beverages from the plane, so, if she finds any, she will have brought it aboard herself." His voice turned playful. "Think you can keep your breakfast down?"

"After four people bail out of a plane with two parachutes, and *survive*, I don't think I have any more airsickness left in me, smartass."

Joey was laughing hard when he disconnected the call.

"GIVE ME THAT FLASH drive!" said the sheriff. He reached out and grabbed the drive out of Addison Slade's hand.

Slade smiled. "Nice, sheriff. That's only a copy. I have several more."

The sheriff looked taken aback at this information, as if it hadn't occurred to him that Slade had made copies.

"Never mind that!" The sheriff was blustering. "I'd say that we need to watch this thing. There might be information on it that we can use."

"I was about to suggest the same thing, Sheriff," said Slade, through a smile.

"*We* own this place?" asked Brandon, flipping a thumb between himself and Patty.

Slade nodded. "You do. Normally, I would have waited until this thing has been probated before I told anyone, but Homer has a few things to say on there that may be relevant to his murder. And he has specific instructions to you two. This time, I thought it would be best to watch it as soon as possible." Slade turned to Sheriff Josephs. "Besides, your tech people need to work on the crime scene. Correct?"

Looking peeved, Josephs nodded.

"Well. That's settled, then. Mr. Brown?"

"Yes, Mr. Slade."

"Is there a compatible computer that we can use that can give us all complete privacy? I don't think word about ownership needs to leak out just yet."

"Yes, sir. There's one in the employee lounge. We keep it in there for employee use. They work some long hours here, and we'd like for them to keep in touch with their social media. We can use it, as long as we keep the door locked."

Slade looked at Josephs again. "Shall we?"

Josephs pulled his gun belt and pants up, tilting his body from one side to the other as he did. "I believe we'll go watch Mr. Crenshaw's so-called will right now."

"Sounds like a plan," said Slade.

JENNY WAS WORKING THE front desk when a good-looking man with a strong resemblance to a young Tom Selleck walked in. She watched as his head turned slowly left-to-right, and his eyes seemed to take in everything. She saw his eyes pause briefly at the doors to the casino, and as they continued to the other side of the lobby.

The man nodded to himself as if the place met his standards, and then he came to the desk.

Jenny felt a tingle inside. Something about this man just made her...

"Hi! Welcome to Big Daddy's! Do you have a reservation?" said Jenny.

"No. No, I don't. I'd like a room, please," said the man. He smiled a hundred-watt smile at her, and his teeth actually twinkled in the light.

"Of course, sir. We have several available. Will you be staying...alone?" Jenny smiled a coy smile.

The man smiled back. "Yes. I mean, as far as I know. Do you have single rooms?"

Jenny nodded slowly. "We do. May I have your name?"

"Oh!" said the man. "My name's Jim Dandy. I'm looking for two of my employees, too. I understand they're staying here."

"Very good, sir," replied Jenny. "If you can tell me their names, I can tell you if they're here or not."

"Right! Sorry. Brandon King and Patty Ferguson."

Jenny's smile faltered the tiniest bit. "Oh. I see. So, you're with Justice Security?"

Jim nodded. "I am."

"They're in the employee lounge," said Jenny. "Which has suddenly become unavailable to employees." The snark in her voice was apparent.

Jim handed over his credit card to secure his room, and Jenny entered the information. Once that was complete, Jim made a request.

"Would you please take me to my people?"

"I can try, but the sheriff might not let you in. Please follow me."

Jenny led Jim to the door that opened into the staff-only hallway, and escorted him to the door to the employee lounge.

"Sir, they're in there. Good luck, and thank you for choosing Big Daddy's."

Jim watched her walk away. Both lust and curiosity guided his eyes. After she left his sight, he knocked on the door.

"IT WON'T TAKE ME A moment to get the computer ready," said Mark Brown.

The table containing the computer had been turned so that it was visible through the room. Brandon and Patty sat next to each other at one of the long employee tables. Addison Slade sat across from them, as did the sheriff.

A knock sounded at the door.

The sheriff shook his head. "I could have sworn we told them to leave us alone!"

The door was behind him, which meant that the two young people were facing it. When the sheriff stood, he crossed to the door and opened it.

Patty saw who it was, hit Brandon on the arm, and vaulted over the table, running to her boss. She threw herself into his arms, and gave her new supervisor a huge hug.

Jim smiled with surprise, and eventually hugged Patty back.

Brandon walked over with a big grin on his face. He reached out, and shook hands with Jim.

Patty pulled away from him and said, "Thank you for coming."

"It's good to see you, Boss," said Brandon.

"Somebody want to tell me who the hell this is?" said Sheriff Josephs.

Patty responded. "This is our boss from Justice Security, Jim Dandy."

"Jim Dandy." The sheriff looked him up and down. "Don't seem like anything special to me."

Jim held out his hand to the sheriff. "Nice to meet you, too, Sheriff."

The sheriff said, "You'll excuse me for not shaking hands." He looked at the two young people. "I suppose you want him in here for this?"

Patty nodded. "We do."

"Ain't that too bad, then? Mr. Dandy, I'm asking you to leave the room. Right now. This isn't your concern."

Patty had had enough. "Mr. Slade?"

"Yes, Ms. Ferguson?"

"Would you allow Brandon and I...for that matter, Justice Security...to hire you to represent us in Carson City?"

"I'd be delighted. You...and Justice Security, by extension...are now my clients."

"Mr. Slade, I'd like for my boss, Jim Dandy, to sit in on this viewing. Can you take care of that?"

Slade said, "Sheriff, my clients have made a reasonable request. Will you honor it, or do I need to advise them to remain silent, and save all of this for the courtroom?"

The sheriff didn't like it. He didn't like it by a long shot. He gave Jim a sour look.

Jim's thoughts centered around one thing. *What is going on here?*

"Fine! He can stay! Brown, are you ready yet?" The sheriff stormed over to the table and stood behind his chair.

"All set. Whenever everyone is ready."

"Patty. Brandon. What's going on?" asked Jim.

Patty took Jim's arm. "Come sit down, sir. It's better if you see it yourself."

Jim followed the young agents to the table, and sat beside them.

"You wanna set the stage for everyone, Addison?" said the sheriff.

Slade nodded once. "Homer Crenshaw was my client for many years. I handled legal work for him personally, and for the casino. Earlier today, I received a call from him. He asked me to come here. He said that he wanted to change his will." He looked at Jim. "He had taken a great shine to your two employees. I just want you to remember that."

Jim nodded his understanding.

Slade continued his explanation. "He had no living family. There is no one that can contest this will. It contains what might be pertinent information about his own murder, the attempt to kill these two young security people, and instructions from him that, as executor of the estate, I intend to see carried out." He nodded to Brown. "Okay, Mr. Brown. You can play it any time."

Brown nodded, and reached over to the computer's keyboard, and pressed a button.

Big Daddy was on the screen.

"Howdy, folks! I'm pretty sure that I must be dead, if you're watching this right now. I'm sorry about any trouble it may have caused, but I wanted to record this today." Crenshaw named the date. "This is my last will and testament, and is witnessed by my shyster there, Addison Slade." Crenshaw chuckled. "Addison is a good friend – hell, he may be my *only* friend! I've also asked him to be the executor of my estate."

Crenshaw sat back in his desk chair. "Well, back to business. I don't have any family, not even a cousin somewhere. I got all this money, and the casino and hotel, and I got only two people to leave it to. Before I say who they are, let me give you a little background on the story." He leaned forward and looked directly into the camera. "If I died as a result of anything besides natural causes, somebody killed me. And that somebody is likely part of the attempts to take over Big Daddy's, and turn it into a brothel...or to grab all the cash. Now, I know those people have their pockets wrapped around the sheriff's hands, so I don't expect a lot of help from him, if I was murdered. So, I'm going to get right down to it."

Crenshaw sighed. "I'm leaving everything I own to Ms. Patty Ferguson and Mr. Brandon King. The whole kit and kaboodle. Every dime that I have anywhere belongs to them. No strings attached, kids, it's all yours. But I do have a couple of things I need for you to do." He held up his hand, with his index finger extended. "One. I want you to find out who killed me." He lifted a second finger. "Two. Somebody that works for me is helpin' those people out. I'll name those people in a minute, but find that inside person!" He lifted three fingers. "Three. Please pay Addison a decent fee for being my executor." He spread his hands. "That's it. You kids work for Justice Security, and they're some good folks. Hell, hire them to come help you find out them two things, if you want to!" He leaned into the camera again. "But I got a feelin' they'll help you two out anyway, 'cause they *are* good folks, and they think a lot of you two."

Crenshaw leaned back in his desk chair again. "Now, let's talk about those people that tried to force me to make Big Daddy's into a brothel. My thoughts on brothels are my own, so I won't share them. But I don't believe that adding that to Big Daddy's would benefit anything, and I will not add that particular service here, even though it's legal, just like gambling. Gambling with money is one thing, gambling with someone's life for sex seems too much like slavery to suit me." He paused. "Well, kiss my grits – I wasn't gonna get into that, and here I am doin' it. Sorry."

He looked directly into the camera and adopted a strong, serious tone. "The people that made the threats belong to a gang. It's Hispanic, and the leader is a man nicknamed Rattlesnake Joe...real name's Jose Guiterrez. He's as mean as a snake, too. He sent three people to threaten me, and I didn't catch their names...but Mark Brown and I did catch them out back, trying to set fire to a couple of our outbuildings! If they didn't go to the hospital after we got through with them, it was only because they didn't want to explain anything to the sheriff! The gang calls itself the Carson City Rattlers, and they're spun off of some L. A. gang. They're into the usual gang crap, like drugs, guns, and hookers. If Sheriff Josephs' hands aren't full of those people's money, I'll eat my hat."

He leaned into the camera again. "On top of that, they got somebody workin' for them inside of my hotel. I don't know who, but I'm pretty sure that it's not Mark Brown. Well, as sure as I can be, anyway. I might be wrong. But I doubt it." He shrugged, and then leaned back again. "But, well, it's *your* hotel now, kids. Just be careful!" He stopped, as if he was thinking. "Oh, yeah, Brandon – it's no fun beating the house when you *own* the house!" Crenshaw burst out laughing, and he waved at whoever was recording. It shut off.

One by one, each head turned to look at Sheriff Josephs. And, as each head turned in his direction, his face got a shade redder.

Finally, he slapped the table in front of him. "CSI units will be combing the office until I say otherwise. It's off limits to everyone until then. Even the new owners." He abruptly stood, and left the room.

Jim turned to Patty and Brandon. "He left you everything?"

"Sir, we're as surprised as everyone else," replied Brandon.

Patty turned to Slade. "Mr. Slade, exactly what can we do with this place?"

Slade thought about it before answering. "The will really needs to be probated, but, honestly, you can do anything you want. It's all yours. There's also quite a bit of money involved, too."

Both young people's eyes widened.

"How much, sir?" asked Brandon.

Slade named the figure. It had eight digits.

As the two struggled to let that number sink in, Jim spoke up.

"Mr. Slade, I want to assure you that Justice Security will take care of any legal fees involved..."

Patty interrupted him. "Excuse me, sir, but the company won't be paying any legal fees. I hired Mr. Slade to represent all of us, and Brandon and I will take care of the bill."

Jim's mouth moved, but no sound came out.

Wow, he thought to himself.

Mark Brown had been quiet during the entire affair. "I would like to offer my resignation."

Brandon looked surprised. "What in the world for?"

Brown looked puzzled. "I'd like to resign before you fire me."

Now it was Brandon's turn to look puzzled. "Why would we fire you?"

"Well, after the way I spoke to you on the day we met, I just assumed..."

Brandon smiled. "Mark. Our old supervisor, Tony Armstrong, always said to never assume. It makes an *ass* out of *you* and *me*. If we have a problem with you, we'll let you know, okay? You're doing great here."

Brown looked relieved. "Thank you."

Brandon waved him off. "It's a non-issue, brother. Let there be peace between us." He held his hand out to Brown, who smiled and extended his own hand to shake.

A knock came from the door to the lounge. Everyone looked at each other with surprise.

Brandon stood and went to the door. When he opened it, a familiar voice said, "Okay, you little shits, what have you gotten yourself into now?"

Brandon started laughing, and swung the door all the way open.

Tony Armstrong stood there, holding a battered military duffel bag.

Chapter 7

The first thing that Tony saw was Jim Dandy sitting at the table beside Patty. The second thing he saw was Patty jumping over the table and running toward him. The third thing he saw was Patty leaping into his arms to give him a hug.

"Oh, Tony, I'm so glad you're here!" she exclaimed.

Tony, smiling, hugged the young woman back tightly. "I couldn't leave my adopted kids all alone during this, now, could I?"

When Patty finally let go of Tony, he shook hands vigorously with a grinning Brandon.

"Hi, Tony! Glad you could make it!"

"I had to come." Tony nodded his head in Jim's direction. "And I see that I'm not the only one that didn't want to leave you two alone out here."

Jim stood, walked around the table, smiled his one-hundred-watt smile, and shook Tony's hand. "Glad you're here, Tony. Did Joey send you?"

Tony shook his head. "No, sir. I'm on vacation."

Jim rolled his eyes. "Now, where have I heard *that* before?"

Patty giggled.

Brandon said, "Tony, you'll never guess what we've inherited!"

"Hmmm...case of the clap?"

Brandon shook his head. "No! Of course not!"

"Maybe...a cow?"

Patty looked incredulous. "Who told you?"

Tony looked surprised. "I was joking, kid. Although I did see a cow out front."

Jim said, "That's Patty's new friend."

"And we've inherited Big Daddy's, too!" said Brandon.

Tony looked very surprised. "Okay, somebody fill me in on what's going on...I came to help, and, now, I'm not sure you need it!"

Patty linked her arm into Tony's. "Come on, Tony. Come meet some people."

Tony was introduced to Mark Brown, and to Addison Slade.

"Now, what's this inheritance talk?" asked Tony.

"Wait until you hear it," said Jim. "You won't believe it, either."

Brandon said, "Mr. Slade, would you please explain it all to Tony?"

Slade smiled. "Of course."

THE PHONE CONVERSATION was brief.

"They're back. Leaving them stranded in the desert didn't work."

"Then we will have to try something else, won't we?"

"But what? We can't risk killing anyone else!"

"We won't have to. Here's what we're going to do..."

"OKAY, SO YOU OWN A casino. And a hotel. Does that mean that our rooms are free?" asked Tony.

Brandon started laughing. "Yes, Tony. And we can give you some casino credit to play with, too. Right, Mark?"

"Yes, sir, we can."

Patty yawned. "I don't know about the rest of you, but it's late, and I'm exhausted. I think I'll check on Flame, and go to bed." She stood up. "Jim, Tony, thank you for coming. You've made my night just by showing up. Good night."

Everyone told Patty good night.

She left the room.

Brandon said, "Tony, I have a request for you...and Mark, I don't want you to take this the wrong way like you did with me..."

"I can't say I'm sorry enough times, Brandon. I feel bad about that," said Mark.

Brandon smiled. "Here's your chance to make up for it. Tony, would you mind terribly if I asked you to shadow Mark for a couple of days? Nothing bad intended, Mark, but I trust Tony's eyes. If he says everything is great and up to speed, then I'll feel better. If this place is ours now, I want it to be the best that it can be."

Mark nodded. "I understand, and I would welcome his advice."

Brandon turned to Tony. "Do you mind?"

Tony smiled. "Kid, nothing would please me more! Gives me something to do in this godforsaken desert!" He shook his head. "I thought I had seen the last of deserts after the Gulf War. That's what I get for thinking!"

"Brandon, what do you need from me?" asked Jim.

"Sir, I need your eyes, ears, and experience. You're right, we need help here. I want to find out who killed Crenshaw before that slapstick clown of a sheriff. You're our best chance of that."

Jim smiled at Brandon. "Anything to help out." He paused. "Will you and Patty still be coming to the new place with me?"

Brandon sat back in his chair. "I hadn't thought about it, sir. And I'm sure that Patty hasn't either. We've only known for what, an hour or two? I don't know about her, but I'm still processing it."

THE TWO VALETS (*my employees now...gotta remember that. Jeez!*) had moved Flame around to the back, beside one of the outbuildings. They had set up a washtub full of water, and had found a bale of hay somewhere. Flame wasn't tied up, and that convinced Patty that the cow truly thought of herself as a pet.

"Hey, girl," said Patty gently.

Flame lifted her head, and made a contented noise. Patty smiled, and began to scratch behind the longhorn's ears. She had to remember to get a currycomb, so that she could run it along Flame's sides, and maybe scratch a few other itches along the big animal's back and sides. She could also fluff up her tail and get the tangles out.

Patty hugged the cow's neck, and ran her hand along the animal's face several times, smoothing out the light fur there.

"Going to bed now, girl. You'll be safe here, and I'll see you in the morning, okay?"

Flame mooed lightly. Patty kissed the cow's forehead, and went inside the hotel through the front lobby.

The noise from the casino was loud and clear as a guest opened the door, but Patty wasn't concerned with it. She was heading for her room, and that was all that was on her mind. She got to the suite she was sharing with Brandon, and took out her electronic key.

Patty unlocked the door, opened it, and stepped inside. After the door shut behind her, she looked up, and was startled.

Someone was in the room, standing in front of her.

Patty's eyes widened in surprise, and she had time to say, "*You!*" Then, something hit her from behind, and she only knew darkness.

"MR. SLADE, WHERE DO you fit in to all of this?" asked Tony.

"I was Homer Crenshaw's lawyer for many years. Now, I'm representing Patty, Brandon, and Justice Security, as long as Justice Security's interests don't interfere with Patty and Brandon's interests. Patty asked first, for both herself and young Mr. King here, so they come first. I will happily represent Justice Security as well, as long as their interests are aligned with these two young people."

Tony nodded. "I understand. But, what I *don't* understand is why this joker left these two everything! He didn't even know them that well!"

"I asked Mr. Crenshaw that same question, Mr. Armstrong. His answer was simple: he said that there was a good feel to these two, and that they deserved it. That was good enough for me," replied Slade.

Tony nodded. "Good enough for me, too, because he was right."

"IS THAT SCRAMBLER WORKING right? I don't want anyone looking at a security camera and see us carrying her out."

"Yes, it's working. Hurry!"

FLAME WAS CONTENTEDLY munching on a mouthful of hay when she caught a scent in the air.

It was Patty's scent.

Flame waited for a few minutes, waiting for her mistress to come and scratch behind her ear again, but she didn't come.

Puzzled, the big longhorn began walking toward the scent. She was just in time to see two people put her mistress into the back of a jeep. The two people climbed inside, started the vehicle, and drove away.

The mighty beast was concerned. She began following, breathing in the scent of both her mistress, and the scent of the vehicle that took her away.

IT WAS LATE WHEN THE chartered jet touched down at the Carson City airport, and even later when Louie and Jessica flagged down a taxi.

"Where to, friends?" asked the taxi driver.

"Big Daddy's, please," replied Jessica.

"Wow. That place is hopping tonight!"

"What do you mean?" asked Louie, as he put their suitcases into the taxi's trunk.

"You folks make the third fare I've carried to Big Daddy's tonight!"

Jessica looked at Louie. "Do you mind terribly if we ask what those two fares looked like?"

"I don't see what it would hurt. The first man looked like a young Tom Selleck, no kidding! I thought it *was* him for a minute, until I saw how young this guy was."

"And the other fare?" asked Jessica.

"He was ex-military, very stern. He managed to look worried, and like he had just eaten a lemon. He commented about being in the desert again, but I don't know what he was talking about." The driver closed the back door for Jessica.

Louie had thrown his head back and was laughing. To Jessica, he said, "You know who they are, don't you?"

Jessica was smiling broadly. "Of course. Tony and Jim."

"Damn kids ain't ever gonna learn to do anything on their own!"

"And whose idea was it to come and check on them, you big hypocrite?"

Both partners started laughing again.

As they drove along the highway, the driver commented, "Well, I'll be damned! Look at that!" He was pointing out the driver's side of the taxi.

A longhorn cow was walking along the shoulder of the highway, going in the other direction.

Louie and Jessica turned around in their seats, and watched the cow plod along in the taillights' reflection until the darkness swallowed it.

THE GROUP IN THE EMPLOYEE lounge finally began to call it a night. They came into the lobby as a group, still talking among themselves. Tony was talking with Mark Brown, and Brandon was listening in. Addison Slade and Jim Dandy were deep in conversation.

Wesley Marlor, the overnight hotel clerk, was at his post. The group stopped by, and Brandon told Wesley that the two rooms being used by Tony and Jim were to be comped.

"Excuse me, Mr. King, but I'm afraid I can't do that."

Slade had followed Brandon to the desk. "Wesley, actually, you can. Mr. Crenshaw left the hotel to Mr. King and Ms. Ferguson. You'll be taking orders from them now."

"Ah, I see, Mr. Slade! Thank you. No one had informed me. I apologize, Mr. King. I'll pass the word along to the staff, so that there won't be any further question about it."

Slade nodded. "Thank you, Wesley. Just make certain that Mr. King's instructions concerning those rooms are followed, please."

"Yes, sir."

"How de hell we 'sposed to get good service around here?" boomed a loud voice from the front entrance.

The group whirled around. Brandon's mouth dropped open, Tony smirked, and Jim shook his head as he smiled.

"I don't believe it!" said Brandon. "*Louie! Jessica!*"

"Hey, kid, we heard you were in trouble. Whose ass needs kickin'?" said Louie through a huge smile. He grabbed Brandon's hand and shook it.

"Normally, I would try to contain Mr. Washington, but not in this instance." Jessica shook Brandon's hand, too. "*Does* someone's ass need kicking?"

Brandon was grinning like a hyena. "No, ma'am, not that I know of. Unless it's the sheriff. *Man*, I'm glad ya'll are here!"

Jim shook hands with Louie, and then with Jessica. "Me, Tony, and now you two. I guess we're all worried about the kids, aren't we?"

Louie grinned broadly. "Hey, man, these kids are the future. Gotta let 'em know they got backup!"

"Brandon, where's Patty?" asked Jessica.

"She went to pet her new pet cow and to go to bed."

"Did you say 'pet *cow*'?"

Brandon grinned broadly. "Yes, ma'am, I did. Let me get you guys a room, and I'll explain everything."

"THIS SHOULD BE FAR enough. We're far out enough out into the desert."

"Yeah, and they rode a damn cow into town the last time."

"No cows out here that I can see."

"Let's just go another few minutes, and then we'll dump her."

"Why don't we just kill her outright?"

"Because we still have the other killing to deal with. Snake killed Big Daddy, and we don't want to have to pay off the sheriff for another killing...or two. If we dump her out here, and the desert gets her, no payoff necessary, because we didn't kill her."

The two people drove in silence for another couple of minutes. They stopped the four-seat dune buggy they were driving beside a clump of rocks, and climbed out. They reached into the back, pulled Patty from the back seat, and left her in the sand.

"Hell, she may not wake up from that bump on the head!"

"Let's go."

The pair got back into the dune buggy and drove away.

Patty, unconscious from the blow to the head, was curled up on her right side in the quiet, nighttime desert sand. A snake, a sidewinder, eased up beside her for warmth, and eventually slid away, as its host shivered a bit in the night air. A breeze blew a lock of her blond hair over her face, and still the young woman slept on, blissfully unaware of what had happened to her.

Chapter 8

"**Y**ou two are the fourth fare going to Big Daddy's tonight...or, rather, this morning," said the taxi driver.

"The fourth?" asked Dexter Beck.

The taxi driver grunted with effort as he lifted Megan's suitcase into his trunk. "Yep, you're the fourth. I suppose you want to know what the others looked like, too...that's what the big black guy asked, anyway." He stopped to think for a moment. "Or was it the blond lady with him?"

Megan smiled at Dexter. "So, sweet husband, looks like we aren't the only ones worried about the children."

Dexter returned the smile. "No, it doesn't." He turned to the taxi driver. "Did the big black guy or the blond lady mention the names of the other two fares?"

The driver held the back door open for Megan, and nodded at Dexter. "She did. I believe she said Jim and Tony. Does that ring any bells, sir?"

Dexter laughed. "It does indeed, sir, it does indeed." He held his hand out to the driver, who shook it. "And if anyone follows behind us, our names are Dexter and Megan."

The taxi driver smiled back. "Mine's Herb Salkowicz. Nice to meet you!"

"SO, THAT'S EVERYTHING that I know," finished Brandon.

Everyone was seated in one corner of the lobby, close to the huge fireplace.

Jessica shared a look with Louie.

Louie turned to Brandon. "What did this cow look like again?"

Brandon described Flame once more for everyone.

"We saw one that looked just like her going in the opposite direction from us as we came here from the airport," said Jessica.

Brandon's face was puzzled. "Away? But she's outside, around the back of the building. Close to the outbuildings."

"You sure?" asked Louie.

"No, but I'll find out. Mark, will you come with me?" Brandon rose from his chair and walked to the front desk.

Mark Brown stood and followed his new supervisor.

Jim asked, "Jessica, do you think it's the same cow?"

"Maybe...likely."

"But why would the cow leave? It obviously had feelings for Patty. And, based on Mr. Slade's story of her original owner, I don't really think that she'd just wander away on her own," replied Jim.

"Perhaps something made her leave," said Slade. "Something...or someone...could have chased her away."

"If that was the case, they obviously don't know Patty very well," said Tony. "There'll be hell to pay if that girl finds out something like that!"

Murmurs of *Oh, yeah* and *You got that right* entered their conversation.

The group sat silent for a few moments.

"Gentlemen, I have a bad feeling right now," said Jessica. She was tapping the fingers of her good hand against the cast on her opposite arm.

Louie nodded agreement. "Yeah, so do I."

Tony added, "Something's wrong. I can feel it."

"You guys are just saying that to make us feel welcome, aren't you?" said a voice from behind them.

They whirled, and saw Dexter and Megan standing side by side, holding hands.

"OKAY, MARK, NO ONE has seen Flame lately, and she's gone. What can we see from the cameras?" asked Brandon urgently.

Mark thought for a moment, with his finger stroking his chin. "Well, we have cameras pointed in that direction." He snapped his fingers. "We should be able to see if anyone messed with her. Come on."

The two men walked down the employee hall to the secure room. Mark ran through the steps to clear himself through the door. When the door unlocked, Mark led Brandon inside.

The men walked to the bank of security monitors. Mark scanned them briefly, then pointed to one.

"That's the one, sir." To one of his seated personnel, Mark said, "Can you rewind number seventeen back about an hour, please? We need to see if Ms. Ferguson's cow wandered off."

The seated man snorted. "Yeah, we saw it take off. It acted like somebody lit a fire under its tail!"

"Rewind it! Hurry!" Mark said with a stern tone.

The seated man shook his head as if he couldn't believe that Mark was taking such an interest in a cow, but he did as he was told. He tapped a few keys on his keyboard, and the image began rewinding. It was hard to watch for something specific, but Mark was used to seeing things at this speed. He had rewound many pieces of video.

"Stop! There!" exclaimed Mark.

The video stopped rewinding.

"Good. Now, play it back. Normal speed."

The seated operator complied.

The monitor showed Flame contentedly munching her hay. It was well lit outside the hotel, so the cow could be seen plainly. She brought her head up, and Patty walked into the camera's view.

Mark, Brandon, and the operator watched as Patty petted the cow, and scratched behind her ears. This continued for several minutes, and then Patty walked out of camera range. The cow settled down to munching on more hay. She continued to munch hay for the next few minutes.

Mark was about to suggest fast forwarding the video, when the cow's head suddenly rose. It was obvious that she was sniffing the air. The cow then began walking slowly toward the rear parking lot, but picked up her pace as she moved. She then disappeared around one of the outbuildings.

"Okay, now I need the video for the rear parking lot. Hurry up!" said Mark.

Brandon said, "It looked as if she smelled something that made her head toward the back."

Mark nodded his agreement. "It did, didn't it?"

The seated man said, "Mark, we had a small problem with the video feed from the back parking lot."

"What small problem?"

The operator squirmed. "We had some kind of interference. It jumbled the video feed."

"And I'm just now finding out about it?" said Mark.

The man squirmed a bit more. "Well, it cleared itself up, and we knew you were busy with the sheriff. We didn't want to disturb you, and we noted it in the log."

Mark looked at the man. "We'll talk about that later. Right now, show me what you have."

"Yes, sir."

The man typed on his keyboard again, and the same monitor began rewinding a different camera view. He stopped it when the video became snow on the screen.

"This is the spot that the video problem began, Mark."

At first, the picture was pure snow. Slowly, bits and pieces of picture began showing through, until, finally, the entire picture could be seen.

Two blurry figures could be seen loading a limp third figure into the back of a dune buggy. The video feed was in color, but the area was dimly lit. All that could be determined was that the dune buggy was a dark color. The two figures that had been carrying the third wore ski masks. By zooming in on the grainy feed, the prone figure could barely be seen. The person was sprawled across the bench-type back seat of the buggy.

The figure had shoulder-length blond hair.

The other two people peeled off their ski masks, but their features weren't clear in the video.

Brandon knew in his heart that the figure with the blond hair was Patty.

"When did this video problem begin?" asked Mark.

"Just a few minutes before the video we watched. And it wasn't so much a when as a where."

Mark's brow furrowed. "What do you mean?"

The operator shifted in his seat again. "Well...it started in one of the monitors outside the guest quarters."

Brandon asked, "Which guest quarters?"

"Yours, Mr. King. And it continued in sequence..."

"...as if someone was walking down the hall and out to the back lot," finished Brandon. "Someone was jamming the signal! And that means..."

"...someone must have kidnapped Patty!" finished Mark.

The operator squirmed even more, as he watched his two supervisors dash out of the room.

He was very worried about keeping his job.

BRANDON AND MARK BURST into the suite shared by the two young Justice Security people.

Brandon ran to the door to Patty's bedroom. He pounded on the door, and called her name. When he heard no answer, he opened the door.

Patty's bed was neatly made. It hadn't been disturbed.

The two men quickly searched the rest of the suite.

There weren't any clues inside the room that they could find.

All the two men knew was that Patty was nowhere to be found.

And that Flame had apparently followed her.

RATTLESNAKE JOE LOOKED hard at the two people standing in front of him.

Jose Guiterrez stood at five feet eight inches. He had black hair, dark brown eyes, and a brownish complexion. His hair was long, and draped to his shoulders. He wore no shirt. He was very muscular, because he worked out with weights for a minimum of three hours a day. Two long scars were visible across his chest from a long-ago knife fight. Guiterrez had won that fight, and now led the Carson City Rattlers as a result. He had several tattoos, three of which were teardrops at the corners of his eyes – one on the left and two on the right. Those teardrops represented the gang-related killings he had done in Los Angeles, long before he had come to Carson City. The fact that his name had been different in Los Angeles, and that he had double-crossed the biggest cartel in Mexico on a drug delivery, weren't relevant to his leadership of Carson City's scariest gang.

But, he had learned a lot from the L.A. gangs. And his feeling that these two should have killed the *gringo* bitch kept tapping the back of his mind.

The two people reporting to him now had convinced him otherwise, however...for now. The sheriff could be a problem, they said, if he had three murders to investigate. He might not be able to cover up that many. It was bad enough that Snake had killed Big Daddy, but no one knew that Crenshaw had changed his will just hours earlier. That ruined up his plan to try to get the hotel/casino from the estate.

At first, Snake just wanted to eliminate the two young Justice Security agents because he didn't want them to snoop around and find out what he was up to. Now, the need to get rid of the two was even more necessary.

"And you're sure she was still out when you dropped her off?" asked Snake.

Both of the people in front of him nodded.

Snake watched their eyes for a minute. Finally, he nodded back.

"Okay, then. Go back to the hotel, and try to drive the other one out to the desert." He shook his head. "I can't believe a damn cow saved their asses the first time!" He looked up at the two people. "You're still here? I thought I told you two to get back to the hotel!"

The two people didn't run, but they did walk briskly as they left.

Once they were gone, Snake gestured to two of his people to come closer.

"Go to the desert. Find the *gringa* bitch. Kill her." As an afterthought, he added, "You can have some fun with her if you want to. But kill her."

Both men smiled broadly in anticipation.

"WHAT ARE WE GOING TO do, Mr. King?" asked Mark Brown.

Brandon was thinking. One of the things that Justice Security had drilled into his head was to handle things on your own whenever possible. But if the situation demanded help, get it.

"The computer feed from the back lot..." It was a statement more than a question.

"Yes, sir?"

"I want you to find Tony and ask him to join you in the security office. Please let him review what we watched. Maybe he'll have an idea of something we can do."

"I'll find him."

"I'm going outside to see if I can make anything out." He glanced at his phone to check the time. "Cripes. It's almost three in the morning!"

"I know, Mr. King."

"Oh, and Mark?"

"Yes, Mr. King?"

"My name is Brandon."

Mark got it, and smiled. "Yes, Brandon."

The two men separated.

As Brandon approached the hotel lobby, he shot a passing glance into the casino. Windowless, lit only by the overhead fluorescents and the flashing lights of the slots, many of the patrons didn't know whether it was day or night, and they didn't care. They played continuously, and stopped only when they were so sleepy that they couldn't stand up, or until their money was gone. He shook his head. He knew that gambling was a nice way to waste a little time, or to have a little fun, but staying open all night was pushing things in his eyes.

His worry about his friend was making him philosophical.

Once in the lobby, Brandon's head was still down, and his eyes were looking at the floor. He didn't notice the group until he reached them.

"What's the word, my man?" asked Louie.

Without looking up, Brandon answered Louie. His tone were distracted. "Patty's been kidnapped. Louie, do you think Dexter would come here if I called and asked?"

"Ask and you shall receive, Brandon." Dexter's soft voice broke through Brandon's distraction, and he looked up.

Brandon's eyes widened as he realized that Dexter was standing there, holding hands with Megan.

"*Both* of you! Oh, *thank* you!" exclaimed Brandon, looking up at the ceiling.

"You say that Patty's missing? What do you need me to do?"

"Come with me, Dexter! Please! And bring Megan! Heck, *all* of you, come with me! I'll take all the help I can get!"

FLAME HAD CHOSEN TO leave the highway.

The cow had followed the road for some way, until she figured out that where her mistress was going. Once she realized the place, which was one Flame had visited before with the longhorn herd, she left the highway and began going across the desert. For her, the going was now easier. Being a cow, she had no way of knowing that the distance was also shorter by going cross-country.

Flame dreamed of having her ears scratched by her new mistress as she walked steadily through the desert.

PATTY, STILL UNCONSCIOUS, dreamed of Flame, and other longhorn cattle, and hay, and pastures full of green grass.

Chapter 9

"Give us more memory, Chandler," said Dexter into the hotel phone. Dexter and Megan Beck sat side by side, with the hotel's computer keyboards manipulating two screens on the wall in front of them. They had called home, and gotten Chandler Hutcheson on the phone. Chandler worked for them in the computer security and information technology department of Justice Security. Through Chandler, Dexter and Megan had initialized a secure encrypted connection with the computer setup at Justice Security.

"Yeah, we're going to need all we can get, if this is going to work," said Megan to Chandler. She was also speaking into a hotel phone, on one of the hotel's landlines. It was the fastest way for the two to connect with the system back home.

"Okay, Becks, we've got both of you loaded up, and you have the entire system at your disposal," said Chandler.

"Great work, Chandler. Can you connect me to Joey, please?" asked Dexter.

"Of course! Hold on a minute." There was a click as the couple was put on hold.

Dexter's fingers were flying on the keyboard in front of him, as he watched the monitor and listened to the phone on the other end ringing in his ear.

"Honey, I've isolated the video footage from outside, and I'm using the video enhancing software. I should have clear, enhanced photos shortly. Once I do, I'll replay it for the people here, and plug photos into some of the facial recognition software." Megan's fingers were also flying across the keyboard.

"Great, sweetie." The call in Dexter's ear connected.

"Hello?" said Misty.

"Hey, Misty. Where's Joey?"

Misty chuckled. Dexter had obviously awakened her. "He's right beside me in a prone position, with a pillow over his head." She giggled. "I put it there. He snores."

In the background, Dexter heard a muffled voice say, "I don't snore!"

Dexter chuckled. "Can you put me on speaker, Misty?"

"Sure." There was a click. "Can you hear us?"

"Oh, yeah, I can hear you fine. Can Joey hear me, or should you remove the pillow?"

"Ten more minutes, Dex! Just ten more minutes, and the alarm would have gone off!"

"Sorry, Joey. I have a reason to call. Patty's missing."

There was silence for a few seconds. "How can she be missing? Where *are* you, Dex?"

"Oh, sorry. Megan and I are in Carson City, checking up on the kids. So is Tony. And Jim. And Louie. Oh, and Jessica's here, too."

Dexter could hear both Joey and Misty. They were laughing.

"What's funny, guys?"

Misty stopped laughing enough to say, "We're stopping there today, too, just to make sure that the kids are alright."

"Good! I was going to ask you to come. Patty's been kidnapped. Megan and I are running some video enhancement software right now to try to figure out who took her. They used some kind of jamming on the security cameras when they took her. I'm going to try some of that new programming that we stole...I mean, that we *obtained* from the NSA, and see if I can remove the jamming from the signal. Remove it from the video feed, if that makes sense."

Joey sounded wide awake when he answered. "I understand, Dexter. Are you connected to our computers downstairs?"

"We are."

"Okay. I'm going to round up Charlie and his new wife, and call Marcus. Once they're all in hand, we'll try to take off and get there as soon as we can. Anything else I need to know?"

Dexter chuckled. "Yeah, Crenshaw left everything he owned to the kids. They're paying our bill. Apparently, they can afford it."

"Oh. Well. That's great. Do they still work for us?"

"From everything I've heard so far, yes."

"Whew. Good. If they weren't, it would have blown the plans for the new place almost totally out of the water!" Joey paused.

Dexter could hear whispering between Joey and Misty.

"Okay, Dexter, we'll be there as soon as we can. You may have to work your magic on Carly again, just so the addiction doesn't attack again while we're there. Send any computer information to the jet when you have it."

"Will do, partner. You guys be careful."

PATTY WOKE GRADUALLY with the rising sun.

The sun shone in her eyes, and her head pounded as if a blacksmith had taken up residence and was running a special on horseshoes.

She sat up, and immediately wished she hadn't. The movement made her nauseous, and she put her head between her knees. She fought against throwing up, and, for a minute, didn't think she was going to win. But, finally, she held her stomach's contents at bay.

For the moment, anyway.

Patty slowly raised her head and looked around. She was in the desert again, but this time, she had no water at all.

Deep shit here, Ferguson. I don't think the cavalry is coming to the rescue this time. I don't know where I am, and nobody saw the people take me.

Suddenly, Patty remembered one of them. The one she had recognized. Remembering, her anger turned into a dull throb in her stomach.

Jenny. The desk clerk. That had been one of the people in her room. Jenny had been the one Patty saw when she entered her room.

Jenny's pretty little face is going to be so much mush when I get back that her own parents won't recognize her.

Patty looked around, and her spirits dropped.

If I get back.

It hurt her head to think, so she just stared at her surroundings.

That slut. Just wait till I get back!

The sun continued its daily trek across the sky, and, with its daily trek, the temperature began to climb.

Oh, God. I bet nobody even knows I'm gone. I do need to get moving, if I'm going to move.

She tried to stand, but her head swam so badly that she couldn't.

Patty pulled herself into the limited shade made by the rocks.

I think I'll take a little nap first.

"KCPX, THIS IS JS-002. We are now entering your airspace. Do you copy? Over."

"JS-002, this is Carson City. We have you on radar. Over."

"KCPX, JS-002 requesting permission to land. Over."

"Copy that, JS-002. You are cleared to land on Runway Ten." There was a pause. "Is this Captain Trotter? Over."

Gena Trotter was the pilot of Justice Security's private jet. Her copilot was David Crews. The company had two jets, but one had been shot down en route to LAX. Gena had been the pilot, and Pat Lambdin had been her copilot. Pat had not survived the crash.

"Yes, this is Captain Trotter. Over."

Gena could hear a smile in the voice on the radio.

"Well, hello again, Captain! We've spoken once before, although you were a little bit preoccupied at the time. Glad to see that you climbed back on the horse."

Gena smiled. The voice belonged to the man in charge of the Carson City tower the day that her plane was shot down.

"How are you? It's nice to hear you again, too. Over."

"Well, I hope you're here for a visit this time, and not an emergency. Over."

"We're only here for a few hours. We're on our way to Los Angeles again. We have people staying at Big Daddy's, and we're stopping for a visit. Over."

Gena could again hear a smile in the man's voice. "That's great! If you have time, please come to the tower. I'd sure like to buy you a soda and shake your hand. Over."

"I'd be glad to. What name should I give? Over."

"Just ask for Cole, ma'am. Everyone knows me. Over."

"I'll do that, Cole, thank you. We're cleared for Runway Ten, correct? Over."

"Yes, ma'am, at your leisure. Over."

Smiling, Gena nodded at her copilot, took the controls, and began her approach.

"MARK, HOW TOUGH ARE the hotel's background checks?" asked Tony Armstrong.

Mark shrugged. "Really deep for people working inside the casino. Not that deep for hotel employees."

Tony nodded. He looked around the security room, with all of its computers, monitors, radios, and communications. "Crenshaw said that the Rattlers had at least one person working on the inside. Any ideas?"

Mark shook his head. "No. Nothing that I can put my finger on, anyway."

"Son, hunches are the biggest asset in our game. Tell me."

Mark snorted. "I do have one suspicion, but I can't be sure. I think that..."

"Hey! We've got one face! Anyone recognize her?" Dexter's voice carried over the noise of the room.

Mark pointed at the monitor. "*She* might be one!"

"Who is that, Mark?" asked Tony.

"Jenny, the evening hotel clerk."

Jim Dandy piped in. "Tony, you remember her! She was at the desk when I got here, and probably when you got here, too!"

Tony peered at the picture on the screen. "You're right, Jim, that's the girl that checked me in!"

A dark look had crossed Louie's face. "Somebody give me her address. I'll go and...*talk*...to her."

"Uh-oh, I'd better come with. I don't like the sound of that, Louie." Jessica's face showed a little concern. "We need her conscious, after all, big guy."

Mark Brown handed a piece of paper to Louie. Louie glanced at it, and said, "Where can I get something to drive?"

Brandon said, "Come with me. I'll get you keys to a hotel jeep." He led the way to the door, with Louie and Jessica following.

"Of course, you can muss her up a bit if you want. Conscious doesn't mean pristine," quipped Jessica.

IT WAS SIX-TEN IN THE morning in Carson City. Joey, Misty, Marcus, Charlie Li, and Carly Stewart were hailing a taxi.

Herb Salkowicz pulled up to the group. His shift ended at seven, so this would be his last fare. He got out of the taxi to assist with luggage, but there wasn't any. He glanced at his passengers, and took a second look at Carly.

"Oh, my God," said Herb. "I never in a million years would have thought that I'd meet someone as famous as you, Ms. Stewart, much less have you in my cab! I'm very honored!" He held out his hand to her.

Carly smiled and, with more grace than she felt, took it. "Thank you, sir. It's always nice to meet a fan."

Charlie held out his hand. "Hi. My name is Charlie Li. I'm her husband."

Herb shook Charlie's hand vigorously. "Sir, I've read about you in the papers! You work for...now, don't tell me..."

"Justice Security?" said Joey.

"That's it! Yeah, Justice Security! How did you know?"

Joey smiled. "I'm Joey Justice. Of Justice Security. We need to get to Big Daddy's as soon as we can."

"Oh, sure! Sure! Right away! That place sure is hopping – I've taken more people out there overnight than I have in a long while!"

Herb moved to open the back door.

Charlie and Carly sat in back, side by side, with Carly in the middle. Misty looked at Joey and smiled.

"Marcus will have to ride in front because of his cast," she said sweetly. "I guess you'll just have to let me sit in your lap, Joey."

Joey's eyebrows moved up and down several times.

Misty laughed as she pulled the taxi's back door closed.

Marcus stood with his crutches, looking at the taxi. Everyone was inside it except him. Sarcasm dripped from his comment.

"It's okay, guys. I can do it all by myself. Thanks for offering your help, though."

STEVE, THE DOORMAN, was walking through the lobby as he passed Brandon, Louie, and Jessica. He overheard them talking about going to pick

Jenny up. He turned and followed them nonchalantly to listen to their conversation. Brandon was talking.

"I believe Dexter will have the other person's face before you guys get back. That software that un-jams a jamming signal is fantastic! Won't the other person be surprised?"

Louie stopped walking. "Listen, son, that software is so secret, *we* aren't supposed to know about it. So don't be talkin' about it, okay?"

Brandon nodded. "Sure, Louie. Any word from Joey yet?"

Jessica said, "They've landed, and should be on their way here."

Steve almost panicked. *If they're going to get Jenny, and if Joey Justice is coming, I need to tell Snake!*

Steve turned on his heel, and left the hotel property quickly.

ADDISON SLADE WAS CONCERNED. He'd always been a well-respected lawyer in Carson City, but he had never represented such a high-profile company as Justice Security. He hoped that he could give them the representation that they needed, and he hoped that he could deliver it with speed and efficiency, and to their satisfaction.

Prudence dictated that he should stay at the hotel until he was certain that his services were no longer needed, and until his client was found. However, that would require some phone calls and schedule manipulation. He looked at Mark.

"Mr. Brown, is there a quiet place that I may use to call my secretary?"

Brown nodded. "Of course, Mr. Slade. Follow me."

Brown led the way to a small office inside the security room. He flipped the light switch, and said, "How's this, Mr. Slade?"

Addison smiled. "This will be fine, Mr. Brown. Thank you. I shouldn't be long."

Brown smiled. "Of course, sir. Please excuse me." Brown left the room.

Addison began making the necessary calls to free up his day.

"YOU SAY THAT JUSTICE Security is here, and that they are on their way to pick Jenny up as we speak?"

Steve's face paled. "Yes, Snake."

Anger flared in Snake's face, but only for a moment. Slowly, a smile spread across his face.

"In that case, we'll give them something...and then, we'll *take*!" Snake took out his cell phone, and made a call.

Jenny answered on the second ring.

"Yes, Snake?"

"Two people from Justice Security are on their way to pick you up. Here's what you're going to tell them..."

THE TAXI CAME TO A halt at the front door of Big Daddy's. Herb jumped out of the taxi, opened the back door, and then ran around the car to open the passenger door for Marcus.

Everyone climbed out of the taxi, and Joey paid the driver. He also gave the man a generous tip.

"Herb, please keep quiet about Ms. Stewart. We're trying to keep a low profile while we're here, okay?" said Joey.

Herb nodded his head vigorously. "Yessir, Mr. Justice. Won't say a word. Thank you for the tip!"

As Herb drove away, Marcus said to the group, "How long do you think he'll last?"

Misty replied to the question. "Oh, at least an hour."

Carly had developed a shake in her hands. It was making her nervous, which, in turn, made her want a drink. "Oh, my God, please help me!" She turned to Charlie. "I don't know if I can *do* this, honey!"

Charlie put his arm around her waist and pulled her close to him. "Of course you can, Carly. Remember, you're the sunflower, and I'm the rose. Pull your strength from me. I'll stay with you as much as I can." To Joey, he said, "Sir, may we please find Dexter? I'm very worried."

"Of course."

The group moved to the front doors, which were held open by two men dressed in jeans, Western shirts, boots, and cowboy hats. They entered the lobby, and were properly impressed by the elaborate Western décor. The door leading to the casino had a brightly lit sign over it, and the word "casino" was written in cursive writing with a three-dimensional tan rope, and a lasso dangled from the "o" in "casino". The door must have been made of thick glass, because they couldn't hear very much of the normal noise that a casino emits.

"Nice place, sugarbuns, isn't it?" Misty asked.

"Very nice," replied Joey. "I hope it stays this way for the new owners."

"I asked for reports last night on Crenshaw, the hotel, the sheriff, and the Carson City Rattlers. The local office has quite a file on Bart Josephs."

"Enough to make an arrest?"

"Yes and no. We could arrest him with what we have, and could probably convict him. But, they're holding off, hoping to catch him red-handed."

"Maybe we can do something about that while we're here."

They had arrived at the front desk.

A young-looking woman, wearing a name tag that read, "Tracy", welcomed them.

"Hi! Welcome to Big Daddy's! I'm Tracy. Do you have reservations?"

Joey smiled. "No, we're from Justice Security. We're looking for Brandon King, or one of the Becks. Can you help us?"

"Of course, sir, just a moment." Tracy picked up the house phone, dialed a number, and spoke quietly into it. When she was done, she hung up the phone and turned back to Joey. "Mr. King will be with you in just a moment, sir."

"Thank you, Tracy." He looked at her more closely, with her black hair cut into a stylish bob that framed her face, her full lips, and her big, green eyes. "I'm sorry, you look very familiar to me. Have we met?"

Tracy smiled at Joey. "No, not that I know of, sir." She shrugged. "I guess I'm just one of those faces. Everyone seems to think they know me."

Joey nodded acquiescence. "I'm sorry. You look very much like a private investigator that I met once. My mistake."

The door marked "WHOA, pardner" opened, and Brandon came out. His face lit up with relief when he saw the group waiting for him. He was smiling broadly as he hugged each of them in turn, and had Carly actually laughing and distracted from her withdrawals.

"Joey, sir, I'm *so* glad to see you guys!" Brandon actually sounded relieved.

Joey smiled. "I don't know why. You've already got most of us here as it is!" They all laughed at Joey's remark.

Marcus said, "Brandon, did anyone from the local FBI office show up?"

"You're damn straight they did!" Brandon laughed. "And right in front of the sheriff, too! They couldn't *wait* to tell him that we were 'duly deputized Federal officers'! I'm telling you, Marcus, you need to angle a raise for those two guys...Tomlinson and Hickerson, I think they said. Yeah, that's their names."

Marcus smiled. "I'll see what I can do, Brandon."

Misty's concern was betrayed by her voice. "Any word on Patty, Brandon?"

Brandon's face turned grim. "Not yet. Thanks to Dexter and Megan, we enhanced the face on one of the kidnappers, and she's an employee here...or, she *was*. I think it's safe to say that she won't be working here again. Louie and Jessica went after her."

Joey nodded. "Good. Would you mind taking us to Dexter? I think Carly needs his services again."

"Oh! Of course! Come on, I'll show you guys the security office – you'll *love* it!"

JENNY DISCONNECTED the call from Snake. Her face had become very pale.

Jenny did not want to go to jail, but that was what Snake told her to do. It frightened her, and made her angry. Who was he to tell her to give up her freedom?

But, had she ever had freedom? She'd been with Snake since he came to Carson City and founded the Rattlers. Before that, she had been with a control freak of a boyfriend, and, before that, her parents had tried to control every aspect of her life.

For Jenny, freedom was an illusion.

And now Snake told her to give up that illusion of freedom for an actual jail cell, made of cement and steel bars. And it would be for quite some time, because kidnapping was serious.

Snake had told her to send the people that were coming for her out into the desert, to the spot that she and Steve had left the girl.

Or else.

Jenny may not have a lot of freedom left in her future, but she at least would have her life...as long as she did what Snake told her to do.

Well...she would do that. But she'd tell them a whole lot more, too.

A VOICE GRADUALLY BROUGHT Patty out of her nap.

The voice had first registered as a dream. Patty dreamed that she was married to Desi Arnaz, and had suddenly turned into a redhead. Her dream was one of her favorite old TV shows, *I Love Lucy*, with herself starring in the show. Desi Arnaz was yelling at her with his funny accent.

"Get up, *gringa* bitch! Wake up!"

At first, Patty didn't understand her dream. Desi Arnaz had never been allowed to say 'bitch' on television in the fifties.

Suddenly, Patty's eyes flew open.

Two men were standing in the limited shade of the rocks, smiling down on her. Both had guns aimed at her – one man held a rifle, and the other had a pair of revolvers, with honest-to-God bandoliers over each shoulder. The taller of the two – the one with the rifle – was wearing a *serape* and a cowboy hat. The shorter man, in addition to his revolvers and bandoliers, was wearing a baseball cap. Both men wore sunglasses.

"Who are you two?" asked Patty, still groggy from being asleep.

The shorter man laughed. "Snake sent us. We're gonna fuck you raw, *gringa*. Then we're gonna kill you!"

Patty hoped that she had enough equilibrium to take these two guys down before that happened, but the way her head was still aching, she wasn't really sure. But, being the woman she was, she couldn't resist smarting off at them.

"I thought a man had to have a dick to fuck someone."

The smiles fell from the men's faces. The short one delivered a vicious kick to Patty's hip as he spoke, timing the kick match his words.

"I said get *up*, bitch!"

Patty yelped. "That *hurt!*"

Shorty kicked her again.

Patty climbed to her feet. As she stood, the tall man put his arms through hers, and linked his hands together at the base of her skull. He had a firm hold on her, and she couldn't move her arms at all.

Shorty smiled again. "Now, we'll show you what we're going to fuck you with, *gringa.*"

Shorty undid his gun belt, and put the revolvers on the ground, next to the rocks. He took off the bandoliers and put them in the same spot. He walked so that he was again in front of Patty. He took off his boots, and unfastened his jeans. He pushed them down around his ankles and stood upright.

Patty looked at what he had, and felt queasy. The man's penis was huge – at least ten inches long, and a good two inches in diameter. Patty decided that this man's penis was coming nowhere near her privates.

"I thought you said you had a dick, asshat."

The smile dropped from the man's face. He pulled his fist back and punched Patty in the stomach as hard as he could.

Patty screamed in pain.

As if it was an answer to Patty's cry of pain, an animal bellowed with anger. From behind the rocks, a huge grey figure streaked toward the short man.

A horn abruptly burst through the man's chest, and knocked his sunglasses off of his head. He was lifted into the air, and was shaken back and forth. The ferocity of the shaking caused the horn to tear through the man's chest.

It was Flame. The longhorn was defending her mistress.

Once Patty realized that the grey figure was Flame, she took advantage of the surprise. She stamped down on the tall man's foot, and bent over quickly, throwing the man over her shoulders. The man's hat flew off, and he landed flat on his back. Patty kicked him in the head with every ounce of strength that she could summon. She heard a crack when her foot connected with the man's temple. He was still breathing, but Patty doubted that he would wake up.

Meanwhile, Flame had trampled what was left of Shorty's body. He was definitely dead.

Breathing heavily, Flame went to Patty and nuzzled her. Patty threw her arms around the big animal's neck and hugged her fiercely.

"Thank you, girl! I thought for sure they had me!"

The cow moved her head against Patty, and rubbed Patty with it. Patty, in turn, began scratching behind the animal's ears.

After a couple of minutes, Patty said to Flame, "Listen, big girl, let's see what we can salvage, okay?"

Patty walked over to the tall man. She stood looking down at him for a moment. Then, she bent over, pulled the man off of the ground enough to pull the *serape* over his head, and let him drop after that. She put on the garment, and then walked over to the man's cowboy hat. She retrieved it, and, to her surprise, it fit her head perfectly.

"How do I look, Flame?"

The cow lowed meekly.

"That's what I thought."

Patty went over to the rocks. She picked up Shorty's bandoliers and holsters, and put them on herself. She also picked up the tall man's rifle.

"Flame, I feel like Megan with all of this crap on!"

A sudden thought hit her. *How did these two get out here?*

Patty began looking around. When she went to the other side of the rocks, she had her answer.

A dune buggy was parked there. Inside, she found four bottles of water. Patty shrugged, and took them. There was also a length of nylon rope. She took that, too.

She debated with herself as to whether she should take the dune buggy, but it would mean that she had to abandon Flame. Patty shook her head. *I just can't do that.*

As she started back around the rocks, she stopped, whirled, and drew one of the revolvers. She fired two shots, one each at the back tires, and watched as they deflated. *Now, if that asshole wakes up, he'll just have to walk back to town. Like I did.*

Even with the sound of the shots, Flame stood patiently, waiting for her mistress.

Patty reloaded the revolver, holstered it, and used the rope to tie a makeshift halter for Flame.

Patty then hauled herself onto the big animal's back, put the rifle across the animal in front of her, took the guide ropes, and began riding the cow back to town once more. She took one glance back, and saw that a couple of circling buzzards had already landed, and had claimed part of the torn body of Shorty. She shrugged to herself, and turned her thoughts toward getting back to Carson City.

Three people are going to pay. This Snake character, Jenny, and whoever hit me on the head. Time to let them know that it's not smart to mess around with Patty Ferguson!

Chapter 10

Gena Trotter waited patiently at the base of the control tower. Airport security rules did not allow her to enter the tower, but she was able to use the phone beside the door to call up. When she did, the person that answered the phone told her that "Cole" would be right down.

Cole. Hmmm. Nice name. I hope he's as nice as his name.

Gena unconsciously smoothed her short, dark hair and ran her tongue over her teeth to make sure that she couldn't feel any trace of the fruit that she had for breakfast. She thought that she might have coffee breath, so she popped a breath mint into her mouth.

Gena was five-five-and-a-half, and was built like most women in their mid-thirties...although she was a bit more muscular, thanks to the stiff Air Force training that she had endured. She was, however, proud to say that she still hit the gym at least once a week, and she took one of Dexter's martial arts classes every two weeks. Justice Security's staff physician, Dr. Orval "Call Me Buddy" Bishop, had pronounced her healthy and back to normal after the recent plane crash that had killed her friend and co-pilot, Pat Lambdin. Dr. Bishop had actually told her that she needed to get back to flying as soon as possible, and Dr. Caleb Mitchell, the Justice Security staff psychiatrist, concurred.

It was sheer coincidence that her first flight, after being shot down in the company's other private jet, was back to the same city that had helped her after the crash.

And, now, the air traffic controller that had been on duty during that incident wanted to meet her.

He'll probably be short, fat, and a total jerk.

Gena sat in the reception lounge, waiting, and hoping that her body wasn't betraying her nervousness.

Gena had made the rank of Captain in the USAF, and had married a man that carried the same rank. Their marriage had been a disaster. The constant stress of military life pulled them into opposite directions. They never spent any time together, and had to rely on fast phone calls and occasional Skype visits. When, through some miracle, they were together for any length of time, they argued constantly. Then, she found out that he had not been faithful. The marriage had ended as quickly as it had started, with each taking with them only what they had brought into the marriage.

Now, Gena felt as if she were trying too hard to be single. It wasn't that she wouldn't tie the knot again, if the right guy came along...but she wasn't giving anyone the chance to become the right guy.

When the plane had been shot down, and she had no choice but to crash-land in the desert, it pounded home the fact that life is fleeting...and that she needed a foundation.

She had part of that foundation already. Justice Security had hired her straight out of the military, and given her a definite flying job. The money was great, the perks were above-and-beyond, and the availability of training for anything she might need in her job all made for the perfect job.

The other part of the foundation? Well, that remained to be seen.

A door on the far end of the reception area opened. A man came through. He had dark hair, a neatly trimmed mustache, rimless glasses, and a nice Western-themed shirt with a string tie. He was about six feet tall, and he was about the most handsome man Gena had ever seen.

The man looked over at Gena, and his face broke into a bright smile. Eyes twinkling, he came to her with his hand out and drawled, "You must be Captain Trotter. I'm Cole Nelson. Nice to meet you."

Gena stood and took Nelson's hand. *Well, hel-lo, Foundation!*

"THAT'S ALL I KNOW, I swear! I can take you to the spot where we dumped her!" Jenny's voice quivered with fear, and she was cowering in the shadow of Louie's huge mass.

Louie hadn't threatened Jenny. He hadn't touched Jenny. He had just *loomed.* And that was enough.

He was the biggest man that Jenny had ever seen. Trained since birth to be either compliant to men or to be beaten, she quickly told Louie and Jessica where the two of them had dumped Patty.

Jessica, sensing the fear pouring from Jenny's pores, said, "Louie, would you please step outside and call Dexter? Please tell him that the other person in the video is Steve, the doorman."

Louie looked at Jessica with raised eyebrows.

Jessica nodded slightly.

Louie took a deep breath. "Okay, Jessica, if you say so. I hope that's everything this girl knows." He glared at Jenny, then stepped outside the small apartment.

Jessica spoke calmly. "Jenny? He's gone. Is there anything else we need to know?"

Jenny shook her head.

"Are you willing to take us to this Snake person's location?"

Jenny nodded.

"If I convince Brandon and Patty not to press charges, would you be willing to come with us, and let me help you start a new life?"

Jenny shot a glance at Jessica.

"Where?"

Jessica smile a small, tight smile, and named the city that housed Justice Security.

Jenny's face brightened. "You would do that for me?"

Jessica sat facing Jenny. "Jenny, I'm a very good judge of people. So is my partner, Joey Justice, and his fiancé, Misty Wilhite. Now, I'm not saying that you won't have to do some major sucking up to Patty Ferguson, but I'm fairly certain that I can convince her to agree to my plan. I'm getting a feeling from you that you're really a good person, but that you've been misused by men most of your life." She met Jenny's eyes. "Am I making a correct assumption?"

Jenny's face showed embarrassment. She looked down, and then nodded.

Jessica's voice turned businesslike. "Then I have your word that you'll help us, and that you'll do your best when we get back to the city?"

"Y-yes."

Jessica smiled, and held out her hand. "Then, come with me, and I'll introduce you to Carly Stewart."

Jenny's eyes widened. "Carly *Stewart?*"

Jessica laughed. "That's right. She's married to one of our people...Charlie Li. They're at Big Daddy's right now." Jessica shook her head in disbelief. "And she's another one."

"Another one?"

"Doing her best to overcome a huge mistake. Just like you. Now, let's go, and let me show you what a big teddy bear Louie really is."

PATTY RODE SILENTLY on Flame's back.

Flame walked. She was in no hurry as long as her mistress was in no hurry. She was content to plod along the desert on the way back to the place her mistress lived. Unless her mistress decided that she wanted to go another route, Flame was taking the desert path back to the hotel. Following that path would bring the least human contact, and Flame sensed that Patty didn't want to be seen until it was absolutely necessary.

As they walked through the desert under the hot sun, they passed some other longhorns, bunched together in twos and threes. All had been abandoned by their owners.

These other longhorns watched as Flame walked past, with Patty on her back. They knew that Patty was a human, but they also saw that Patty was causing no harm to Flame.

Overcoming its curiosity, one steer began following Flame quietly.

Patty, dozing in the morning heat, didn't notice the new traveling companion.

Soon, another longhorn walked with them. And another.

All of them were heading for Big Daddy's.

And all of them followed Flame.

"OKAY, LOUIE CALLED and said that Steve isn't at home. Where else would he be?" asked Joey.

Brandon looked down. "I don't know, Joey. I'm feeling lost right now...can't think."

Tony studied Brandon. "C'mere, Brandon. I need to talk to you."

Tony pulled Brandon to a quiet corner of the security room. Joey followed. "Okay, spill it. What's wrong?"

Brandon shook his head. "I'm worried sick about Patty. I don't know what to do."

Tony crossed his arms. "That doesn't sound like the Brandon I know."

"Maybe this *is* the Brandon you know. Maybe I don't function well when my best friend is missing, or maybe dead."

"If I thought that, I wouldn't have told the boss here that you were ready for this new job. Now, focus and *think*, dammit! Patty's counting on you, and you've been here longer than we have!"

Brandon allowed himself to tune everything else out. He focused his mind inward, actually studying the situation.

Joey watched the younger man. He was delighted to see that Brandon was attempting to be proactive instead of reactive.

Brandon's eyes swam back into focus, and he became very businesslike. He turned to Joey.

"Did Jenny provide Louie and Jessica with the address of the Rattlers hideout?"

Joey uncrossed his arms, and put them to his sides. "She did."

"Sir, did Megan bring any weapons?"

"Probably. You know Megan. If she didn't, we have Marcus."

"Then here's my suggestion, sir. We load up, all of us, and go take the Rattlers down. Hard."

Joey smiled, and patted Brandon on the shoulder. "*There's* the man I hired!"

Brandon smiled back, and turned swiftly. "Mark! We're heading out! You're in charge of the hotel!" He turned to Addison. "Mr. Slade, will you stay here and help him?"

"Of course, Brandon. It would be my pleasure."

"Mark! Mr. Slade is staying to help you!"

"Yes, sir!"

Brandon turned to Joey. "We'll take the hotel jeeps. Do we need to go to the airport for the weapons?"

"Let's find out."

"AND THAT'S MY STORY, Gena. Divorced, no kids, and a damn good job."

Gena and Cole were sitting in a small diner, having breakfast and coffee. The conversation had been wonderful, and the couple found that they enjoyed the other's company. A lot.

"My story is basically the same, Cole. I married a man in the military, same rank, but a different unit. We really thought we could make it work, but the stress of being apart all of the time...well, let's just say that it doesn't promote fidelity. We divorced, and when I left the Air Force, Joey offered me this great job flying the Justice Security jets. It's great. I don't have to go very often, but I do have to sometimes be on call. It pays really well, and I get plenty of free time."

Cole smiled at her. "And you sometimes get shot down, too, right?"

"That was my first time for that, I'll have to admit. And I lost a friend. It wasn't a fun thing."

"I can imagine." Cole sipped coffee, and met Gena's eyes. "And I just happened to be the controller on duty that day. I can't say that I've ever had the experience, either." He put his mug down on the table. "You do realize what a great job you did, don't you? You survived, your passengers survived...and if the rescue people had gotten there even ten minutes earlier, your co-pilot would have survived. That's some damn good flying, Gena! And I'm proud to finally meet you."

Gena blushed as she spoke. "I can't think of anyone else that I'd rather be with right now."

Cole smiled back. "I can't, either."

Gena's smile promised many things, and Cole's smile promised the same.

The anticipation was delicious.

PATTY FOUND HERSELF in the middle of a group of men. They were all talking at once, but they all sounded like cattle.

A sudden bump caused her to wake from her dream. At first, she looked around wildly, wondering where she was. Then, she saw Flame's broad back, and remembered.

But she could still hear the talking that was in her dream. She looked behind her, and saw that fifty to sixty head of longhorn cattle were following her and Flame.

"Flame, we have company."

Flame mooed back.

Wow. I wonder why they're following us?

The cattle didn't seem nervous, and seemed to be happy following her cow.

Patty shrugged. She had inherited enough money to buy a good-sized ranch at the new location, so she could give these cattle a good home.

She turned back around, facing forward. She had no idea how far they were from Big Daddy's, but she trusted Flame to get her there.

As Patty rode, a plan began to form...and she found herself smiling.

Chapter 11

Joey was directing everyone to their places.

They had arrived at the address Jenny provided. Marcus had insisted on calling in some agents from the Carson City office to help round up the Rattlers.

Marcus had not invited the sheriff.

Dexter had hypnotized Carly again before they left the hotel, and she was doing fine once more. She had insisted on coming along, so that she could stay with her husband. Joey had told Charlie that she could come, but only if she stayed out of the line of fire.

Carly had agreed. She seemed enthusiastic about coming along.

Joey hoped that she knew this was real, and not a movie.

The Rattlers' hideout was an old three-story, rundown adobe house, with Spanish architecture. Terra cotta tiles lined the roof, and the tan-colored adobe blocks were chipped and cracked. The ground floor windows were all boarded up with plywood, and nothing could be seen through the mini-blinds on the windows on the second and third floors. The house was on the corner of two streets, and had vacant lots on the other two sides.

Joey's plan was to surround the house, much like they had surrounded the apartment house in Chicago that Esteban Fernandez had holed up in. Then, they would use a bullhorn and demand that the people inside surrender.

It was agreed that Marcus, still on crutches, would stay back out of the line of fire, and would keep track of Carly. Jessica would stay back as well, nursing her broken arm. Joey gave everyone their instructions, and the house was surrounded according to plan. Marcus had the bullhorn, and was prepared to give the announcement.

After a nod from Joey, Marcus put the bullhorn's microphone to his lips.

"Attention, Rattlers! This is the FBI! We have the house surrounded! Come out with your hands up!"

Mini-blinds on the second floor at the side of the house facing the street moved. Misty had that side, along with two FBI agents. Louie, Brandon, and an FBI agent had the side of the house facing the vacant lot. Dexter, Megan, and another FBI agent had the back, and Joey was in the front with Jim Dandy, Tony, and more FBI agents.

Misty's voice came quickly across the radio that each person carried. "Movement on the second floor."

"Any idea on how many are inside?" Louie sounded pissed.

"No intel on that, big guy," Joey replied.

"According to our local people, there could be as many as thirty," added Marcus.

Plywood suddenly flew into the yard from one of the downstairs windows, as if someone had kicked it out. Plywood from another first floor window flew out on the street side.

"Awww, *shit!*" Louie said over the radio.

The first shot was fired from the front of the building, toward the position that Joey and Jim were standing. Both men hit the deck, and Joey opened fire.

Almost as soon as the second shot was fired from Joey's gun, the first floor of the house exploded into a massive fireball.

As burning pieces of the house began falling into the street, Louie's voice again came over the radio.

"Joey, what the fuck did you blow up now?"

TRACY, THE DESK CLERK, looked up as the front door of the hotel opened. She saw Steve coming in...with about twenty or more people behind him. They all had determined looks on their faces, and they made her nervous.

Then she noticed the guns they all carried.

A couple of years earlier, Homer Crenshaw had installed what he called a "panic button" at the front desk, and in all of the booths housing pit bosses in the casino. When the button was pressed, it alerted everyone in the security room.

Tracy pressed the button, then ran down the employee hallway and out of the hotel.

SNAKE LET THE DESK clerk run. After all, she was only a desk clerk. She didn't have access to any cash.

Cash was the reason for this entire thing. Snake wanted cash. The Rattlers gang wasn't high maintenance, but he liked to have cash available for necessities. He tried to convince Crenshaw that prostitution was the way to go, and that there was a big difference between *reported* income and *actual* income...and Snake would be glad to show him how to do it. Crenshaw wouldn't listen, and had thrown Snake out of his office. Crenshaw had humiliated him in front of his people. If he had declined with respect, Snake would have taken it and left the man alone. After all, there were other hotels in Carson City. But, Snake couldn't let the humiliation stand, and Crenshaw had paid the price.

Now, Snake was going to take every last dollar out of the hotel, and out of the casino. After he had it all, Snake was going to burn the place to the ground. With the Justice Security people out of the way, the entire thing should be quick and easy.

Snake directed two of his people to guard the front door. He posted three at the employee hallway. Everyone else went to the casino.

WHEN THE ALARM SOUNDED inside the security room, Mark Brown turned to the monitors.

"Holy *shit*!" he muttered.

"What's wrong, Mark?" Addison had moved up beside Mark.

Mark pointed at the monitors for the front lobby. "Look."

The first monitor focused on the front doors, and two Rattlers could be seen plainly, guns drawn, with one on either side of the door. A second monitor was fed from a camera with a side view of the main lobby, near the front desk. Three Rattlers were fanned out in front of the employee hallway. Their guns were drawn, and they were pointing down the hall.

"People!" Mark called out to get everyone's attention. "We have a *problem!*"

MARCUS HAD TAKEN CONTROL of the scene, and was directing his agents, the city's firefighters, and various law enforcement officials. Sheriff Josephs had arrived on the scene, and Marcus was arguing with the man.

"And I'm tellin' *you* that this is *my* city, and *my* crime scene!" Josephs was two inches from Marcus' face, and was shouting. "And if you have a problem with that, tough *shit*!"

"Josephs, you are about two seconds away from being arrested! Back *off*!" Marcus used his finger to tap the sheriff's chest for emphasis.

The sheriff knocked the FBI chief's hand away, and reached for his weapon. Before his hand got to the gun on his hip, a huge hand fell on the sheriff's shoulder, and squeezed. The sheriff flinched in pain, and his head whirled around to see who had grabbed him.

It was Louie. And he was angry.

Deputies had drawn their weapons and pointed them at the big man. As soon as they did, FBI agents and the Justice Security people drew their weapons, and pointed them at the deputies.

Louie leaned down into the sheriff's face, looked into the sheriff's eyes, and spoke with a fierce voice.

"Tell your people to stand down, you asshole. The first thing that will happen if they don't is that I'll rip your head clean offa your neck. Then, you're gonna listen to Marcus. If he say to jump, you gonna ask how high...but you better be in the air when you ask!"

Louie applied a little more pressure to the man's shoulder for emphasis.

The sheriff flinched, and grunted with the pain.

"Stand down! Holster your weapons!"

The deputies holstered their weapons.

Louie did not let go of the sheriff. But he *did* look at Marcus with expectation.

Marcus nodded his understanding, and spoke to his agents.

"Gentlemen, arrest every one of these men. Charge them with assault on a Federal Officer."

"Yes, *sir*!" replied Agent Hickerson. He was smiling broadly.

Each deputy was disarmed, handcuffed, and had their rights explained to them. Most of the deputies looked amazed at the turn of events, and kept glancing at Sheriff Josephs for explanations.

The fire chief came up at that point, and sized up the situation quickly. He spoke to Marcus.

"Chief Moore, two people were inside."

Marcus stared in disbelief. "Only *two*?"

The fire chief nodded. "Yes, sir. The explosion was caused by a box of old hand grenades. Looks like a bullet hit them, and caused them all to explode."

Everyone turned to Joey.

Joey shrugged. "Oops."

Louie shook his head with amazement.

Marcus shook the fire chief's hand. "Thank you, Chief."

The fire chief smiled. "You're welcome, Chief." He turned to the sheriff. "Bart, it looks to me like your fuckery has caught up with you." The fire chief turned and went back to the still-smoldering house.

Dexter snorted. "Louie, I believe someone has stolen your word."

Megan giggled, and everyone else smiled.

Even Louie.

Louie spoke again. "Marcus, you gonna arrest this asshole? Can I hurt him now?"

Marcus opened his mouth to answer, but the portable radio that the sheriff carried squawked into life.

"All available units please respond. Shots fired at Big Daddy's. Any units in the area, please respond."

Brandon had a look of surprise on his face, then dread. "I have to go. Joey, I have to go!"

"I'll come with you."

Marcus stopped Joey. "You can't. I need you here. This mess is yours, Joey, and you're staying to see it cleaned up."

Jim spoke up. "I'll go with him. The kids are mine now, remember?"

Joey nodded, and waved them on their way.

Dexter raised his eyebrows to Joey, asking a silent question.

Joey said, "No, Dex. Let them handle it. The three of them need to get used to handling things on their own. Together." He paused. "But feel free to worry. That's what I'll be doing."

WHEN PATTY RODE FLAME into the circle driveway in front of Big Daddy's, there were about seventy-five head of unowned longhorn cattle following her. Well, maybe they weren't unowned now...they were hers.

The first thing she noticed was that there weren't any doormen.

Where are the doormen? We always have two at the door. I wonder if something is wrong?

Her question was answered almost immediately when one of the glass doors opened slightly, and a shot rang out. It missed Patty, but she heard the bullet whiz past her left ear.

Patty drew both revolvers, and goosed Flame in the ribs with her heels. As Flame began running toward the doors, Patty fired one shot from each pistol. The two shots broke the glass out of the front doors, and Flame hit the metal that remained a couple of seconds later. The two doors slammed inside when the big animal hit them with her head down, and they banged backwards into the two people guarding them. Both dropped to the floor, out cold. The cattle behind Flame had begun running, too, following the herd leader into the lobby of the hotel.

The three people guarding the employee hallway turned in astonishment, staring open-mouthed at the young woman wearing a cowboy hat and *serape*, and riding a cow. The few seconds of amazement cost the three gang members, however. Patty fired both weapons, and hit all three of the men. They collapsed onto the floor.

Holstering her left gun, Patty swung her right leg over Flame, and jumped down to the floor. She kept the right pistol pointed at the three men as she walked over to them.

Mark burst from the hallway at that moment, followed by Addison Slade and several other security men, and his gun was drawn. Patty almost shot him, and Mark almost shot her. But both recognized each other in time, and held their fire.

Patty indicated the three men by pointing with her gun barrel. "They dead?"

Mark holstered his gun, and knelt beside each. He checked their pulses while the other security men handcuffed the two that had been knocked out by the doors.

Mark looked up at Patty. "Two dead, one is alive. Barely."

Patty shrugged. "Call an ambulance."

"That's not all of them, Patty. There's about twenty or twenty-five more of them in the casino. The cameras showed that they were rounding up all of the cash that's on the gambling floor, and some of them are trying to break into the counting room."

Patty glanced toward the well-soundproofed casino, then looked back at Mark. "Where's Jenny?"

"She's with Jessica Queen. They're at the Rattlers' headquarters. Apparently, it exploded." He paused. "Jenny's partner – the one that hit you – was Steve, the doorman. He's in the casino with the other Rattlers."

Patty's face turned even angrier. Plans raced through her head, and she discarded them one by one, until only one remained.

"Mark, get us some help here. Fast." Patty began reloading. "I'm going in, but I'm leaving the door open just a bit. You stay at the door, and if I need help, I'll call you. Have the Rattlers hurt any of our guests?"

"No, ma'am. The guests are bunched together in front of the poker tables, but they mostly just seem scared. There are four people guarding them."

Patty nodded her acknowledgement.

"What about all of these cattle, ma'am? We can't just leave them here."

Patty turned her face to Mark. The look he saw actually frightened him a little.

"Touch any of them, and I'll break both of your knees."

"Y-yes, ma'am."

"DAMN! JIM, WON'T THIS thing go any faster?"

Jim was driving the jeep, and Brandon was riding shotgun. They were speeding through town. Jim glanced at the speedometer, and they were doing sixty through the city of Carson City.

"It could, but we might hurt someone. Mark is there, Brandon. Don't you think he can handle it?"

Brandon nodded. "I guess so, but it still worries me. Who's firing shots at the hotel? And why?"

Jim had a grim look on his face. "We'll find out when we get there."

"Yeah, I guess so. Jeez, I wish I knew where Patty was right now."

"So do I. We know where, we just can't go get her right now."

"Sucks."

"Oh, *shit*!" Jim slammed on the brakes. The jeep stopped just a couple of feet away from a school bus.

Both men breathed a sigh of relief that they had stopped in time.

"Maybe we should slow down a little," said Brandon.

"Wow, you *think*?" replied Jim.

PATTY GENTLY PUSHED the door open to the casino. The bright lights over the slot machines still flashed with merry abandon, but the gambling sounds that usually accompanied the lights were absent. Instead, she heard sobs and crying from the guests across the room, and occasional shouts from their guards telling them to shut up.

Patty had tucked her hair up under her hat, and walked with her head down, trying to shield her face. She was hoping that the tall man's *serape* and hat would disguise her for a short while, until she saw what was going on.

She had propped open the glass entrance door open with a huge old dictionary that had been on one of the bookshelves in the lobby. It held the door open about eleven-to-twelve inches...enough that Mark could hear her if she called him.

Patty glanced at the guests. One man seemed to have had a bloody nose, and another was lying with his head in a woman's lap, but no one appeared to be seriously injured. One of the guards was Steve, and it took all of Patty's restraint to keep from going over to him and punching him as hard as she could.

A quick count showed twenty-three Rattlers. One appeared to be trying to crack the encryption on the combination for the counting room door. He had what appeared to be a tablet wired to the lock. Patty wasn't worried. It would take hours for them to hit on the correct sequence, even if they had the encryption key. Three others stood around the man with the tablet.

She glanced again at the prisoners, and saw that all of the card dealers and game operators were among the guests.

The Rattlers had taken everyone prisoner.

After one last quick glance around, Patty decided that she had seen all she needed to see. It was time to sneak back out.

As she worked her way silently to the casino entrance and safety, someone called out to her, and she froze.

"Felipe! Where are you going? Did you kill the woman?"

Patty knew that the person calling to her recognized the hat, bandoliers, and *serape*, and thought that they were talking to the man that Patty had kicked in the head.

But, there was no way she could pass for him – she wasn't tall enough – and whoever had called out would realize that in seconds.

"*Dammit,*" she muttered.

With one swift motion, Patty whirled toward the voice and drew both guns. She saw the man that had called her, and snapped off a shot at him as she dove for cover behind the slot machines.

"Mark!" Patty hoped that Mark heard her, and that she didn't sound too desperate. Somebody began shooting in her direction. From the amount of shots fired, it sounded like several somebodies. Glass, metal, and casino tokens flew all around Patty as one slot machine after another was shot to pieces.

Patty was able to see the guests and employees from her vantage point. They had all taken refuge behind some overturned blackjack tables. She could also see the feet and legs of several of the Rattlers, and shot three of them in the leg before she had to move from her position. She didn't get far, however. A man stood in front of her at the end of one of the slot machine aisles. Patty had almost landed against his legs before she saw him. When she looked up, it was into the double barrels of Snake's side-by-side twelve gauge shotgun.

"I should have known those two fuckups wouldn't get the job done," Snake said. He was smiling, and his tone was almost conversational. "Tell me – are they still alive?"

Patty also sounded conversational. "Shorty...Felipe...was killed by my cow, Flame. She gored him. The other...well...let's just say that I left him unconscious in the desert. Just like Steve and Jenny left me." Then she smiled.

The smile abruptly left Snake's face. He swung his right leg, and kicked Patty in the side of the head. She cried out in pain.

MARK HEARD PATTY CALL him, but he also heard about forty shots ring out. A few seconds later, he heard three more shots. He dropped to the floor, and motion for the other three security people to drop, too.

When Patty called out for Mark, Flame's head came up and turned toward the casino doors.

Mark didn't hear anything else.

But Flame did.

"JIM, WHY ARE THERE cows in the drive?" asked Brandon quietly.

About a dozen longhorn cattle were spread out in the circle driveway. Jim couldn't get the jeep any closer to the entrance because of them.

"Interesting question, Brandon," replied Jim. "I wish I could answer you."

As the two men stared at the cattle, Brandon realized that the hotel's front doors were open, and cattle were inside.

"Jim, why are there cows inside my hotel?" asked Brandon quietly.

Jim turned to look. "Hmm. Let's go find out."

As the two men climbed out of the jeep, the cattle abruptly started moving quickly through the lobby.

The men exchanged a puzzled look. As they did, realization slowly dawned on Brandon's face.

"The casino!"

The men began running.

PATTY WAS ON THE FLOOR, stunned from the gang leader's kick.

Snake leveled his shotgun, and aimed it at Patty's head. "So long, *puta*. Enjoy life on the other side."

The casino doors burst open, and Flame ran in at full speed, followed by most of the cattle from the lobby. The old cow stopped and looked around while all of the other cattle tried to stampede through the destroyed gambling hall. She spotted the incredulous Snake, looking at her from ten feet away.

Sensing that this man meant harm to her mistress, Flame lowered her head, and pawed the ground. Her snorts were rhythmic, and with the third one, she charged the still-staring gang leader.

Snake forgot that he was holding a shotgun, and began backing away from the furious longhorn. He wasn't watching where he was backing, however, and his feet slid out from under him when he stepped on a loose pile of poker chips.

Flame reached him then, and the man screamed as one of her horns pierced his chest cavity. Flame gave a mighty bellow, and shook her huge head.

Snake's body ripped in half, and each half fell to the floor.

Brandon, Jim, Mark, and the other three security people ran into the casino to find about seventy longhorn cattle milling around, pinning the Rattlers against tables, doors, and walls. Three had been trampled.

Flame was gently nudging Patty with her nose, trying to get her mistress to stand.

Brandon saw Snake, and walked quietly over to Patty, and knelt by her side. "Easy, Flame. Patty? Can you hear me?"

Patty's eyelids fluttered, and she suddenly opened her eyes. "Brandon! What happened? Where's that guy?"

"What guy, Patty?"

"The one with the shotgun! The one that kicked me!"

Brandon realized that she must mean the man on the floor that Flame had torn apart.

"He, um...kinda went to pieces, Patty. Come on, let's get you up."

He helped Patty to her feet. She looked at Flame's horns. They were again bloody.

"Flame, did you...Brandon, did she...?"

Brandon indicated Snake with a nod in that direction. "Looks like your cow took him out."

"Wow. That's twice she's saved my life." She reached out to the big animal and hugged her around the neck. She put her head against the steer's back and said, "Thank you, girl. Again. And your friends, too."

Chapter 12

A week later, the Justice Security partners were sitting in the lobby of the hotel, waiting for Patty and Brandon.

They had all taken a week's vacation from Justice Security so that they could help the two young people with whatever they could.

The hotel and casino was insured to the hilt, according to Addison Slade.

"Homer had the place so covered with insurance that he could put in a claim for bird droppings, and it would be covered," the lawyer quipped.

The biggest thing they had to deal with was the aftermath of the arrests of all of the Rattlers. When the FBI arrested Sheriff Josephs and the deputies that had been at the Rattlers' hideout, it had left Carson City a little short-handed in law enforcement. Marcus had taken over the agents in the Carson City FBI office, and drafted them for city law enforcement duty...at least until the City Council hired more people.

Patty had shown great restraint in dealing with Steve. He had been one of the people that she shot in the ankle in the casino, but she had given him first aid until paramedics and some kind of law enforcement had arrived. She *wanted* to punch him until her hand hurt, and *wanted* to let him bleed to death, but she couldn't do it.

Both men that had come after her in the desert were dead. The second man didn't regain consciousness before the buzzards had started feeding.

Patty also had come to terms with Jessica's decision to offer assistance to Jenny. Patty had no idea what it would be like to be controlled by men the way Jenny was, but she could empathize with her, and agreed to leave Jenny's name out of any police reports.

Slade had been a godsend for Patty and Brandon. He had "fast-tracked" the probate process by calling a friendly judge, and everything now was fully probated. Brandon and Patty were the official owners of all of Homer "Big Daddy" Crenshaw's property.

Slade had explained to them about the ownership of the property, the insurance covering the destruction of the casino by both the cattle and the Rattlers, and what needed to be done to restore the place. The hotel had not been harmed, with the exception of the lobby, and guests that wanted to stay were welcome at half price. Word had spread through the hotel about the owner facing down a gang, and most guests elected to stay. They felt safe and secure knowing that the staff and owners were willing to go to such lengths to *keep* them safe and secure.

Joey's "Justice Security Vacation Week", as he called it, was over tomorrow. Everyone would be flying back to their own city, and Jim Dandy would be heading to the new site, hopefully with Patty and Brandon, to oversee construction of the new "backup" building. Joey wondered if he would have a pilot, since no one had seen Gena all week. He also wondered if the kids would accompany Jim to the new site. He certainly hoped that they would, as did everyone else.

Tony actually voiced this concern.

"Boss, do you think the kids asked us here to tell us that they were staying here?"

Joey smiled, resignation in his face. "I really hope not, Tony. You know them well. What do *you* think?"

Tony actually thought for a minute. "You know, boss, this is hard one to call. I really don't know."

Tony, along with Dexter and Megan, had assisted Mark Brown with bringing his security systems up to date, and had even enhanced them with a few additional "add-ons" used by Justice Security. Of course, all of the "add-ons" had been very hush-hush, and at no charge. Mark had also been given a direct line to the Justice Security IT room, with computer usage as needed. Tony had shown Mark several safer ways to monitor the building and the grounds, and had made suggestions about security in both the counting room and the security room.

"Mark, you call us any time," Dexter had told him. "If you need something in computer monitoring, you tell us. We'll fix it for you."

"Come to the Justice Security building sometime, too," Megan had added. "We'll train you in hand-to-hand combat, and give you some weapons training, too."

Tony had been more direct. "Look, the kids own the place, so you always got us. You need something, let us know. Somebody will come running."

Charlie Li and Carly Stewart had flown on to the clinic two days ago, although Dexter's hypnotism and a few meditation techniques had been helping Carly with her addictions. Dexter was willing to continue, but Charlie felt that they should see if rehab would do anything better. If not, they would leave and let Dexter continue his treatment.

Now, Tony and all of the partners were waiting in the lobby of Big Daddy's, because Brandon and Patty had asked them to meet them there. All of them had been enjoying the day, and were dressed appropriately.

Tony had gone for an overnight hike in the desert, and had just arrived back at the hotel an hour earlier. Joey and Misty had slept late, and were waiting to go have breakfast. Dexter, Megan, and Louie had been working out, and practicing on some new martial arts moves. Jim had been on the phone with the construction company, making sure that everything was going to start on time. Jessica had stayed up late, calling up a horror movie on the hotel's pay-per-view, which was free to her. She had not had breakfast, either, and was planning to enjoy a late breakfast with Joey and Misty.

Louie happened to see Brandon and Patty, accompanied by Addison Slade and Mark Brown, as they came toward the spot where the partners were sitting.

"Hey, here dey come," Louie said quietly.

Everyone turned to face the four people as they approached. Patty caught Misty's eyes and smiled lightly. Misty smiled back and nodded encouragement.

"Wow. I feel like we've been called up on the carpet," quipped Brandon.

"Have you all been enjoying your stays?" asked Patty.

All of the partners nodded or agreed that they were enjoying themselves. Only Tony was different.

"Look, you two, we're all on pins and needles. What's up? Are you coming back to work or not?"

Brandon looked at Patty. Patty looked at nothing for a moment, and looked back up.

"We've learned what it means to be partners," Patty said. "We know it takes a lot of work, and we're very, very aware of how partners have to rely on each other, and to rely on other people."

Brandon nodded his agreement. "Not just when we're in danger, either. We've had to compromise on things this week, and co-sign things, and you name it."

Patty continued. "Addison told us that at least one of us has to be here to oversee the casino reconstruction. As far as running the casino and hotel, we're giving that responsibility to Mark, once the casino is taken care of and rebuilt." She took a breath. "Now, comes the hard part. Like I said, one of us has to stay for a while."

Brandon spoke up. "We flipped a coin."

"Right. One of us will need a leave of absence, if you guys can see your way clear to granting it."

Everyone was quiet.

Finally, Joey spoke up. "Okay, are we going to be held in suspense, or are you two going to keep us in the dark?"

Brandon and Patty smiled, and Brandon spoke.

"I'll be staying to oversee the casino reconstruction, while Patty goes with Jim to the new site. I'd like to request a leave of absence for as long as it takes. If you're willing after that, I'd like to join Patty at the new place."

"It was a tough decision for us, in all seriousness," added Patty. "In the end, like Brandon said, we had to flip a coin. Brandon lost. Or won. Depends on how you look at it."

Everyone laughed.

Joey looked around at his partners with his eyebrows raised. Each partner nodded as Joey caught their eyes. He nodded back when he had seen each nod.

"We figured that somebody was going to have to stay. We had hoped that it would work out like this, but we were all afraid that you would decide that you both had to stay. But, first, let me say this: Brandon, take your leave of absence. As long as you need to get the casino running, and to get Mark ready. We have been talking amongst ourselves, too, and we've come to a decision. Once the new facility is up and running, we'd like to talk to the two of you about becoming partners in Justice Security." He smiled. "That would give you two partnerships in *two* companies. So, keep that in mind."

Both young people's mouths dropped open. This had been the *last* thing that either of them expected.

Joey continued. "Next, anytime you need help here, for anything, you two don't wait – tell us right away, and we'll come bail you out of whatever you need bailing out of."

Brandon, still reeling from the partnership talk, said, "Thank you, people. You've all been so good to us!"

Misty smiled. "Good has nothing to do with it, Brandon. As we told Charlie and Carly, it's family."

"Even when it's the bloody drunken black sheep," muttered Jessica.

Everyone laughed.

Jim turned to Patty. "Our plane leaves in the morning, then we have a six-hour drive ahead of us. Will you be ready?"

Patty half-smiled. "I'll be there. I'll have to find a nice farm somewhere in the new town, and have Brandon arrange shipping for my livestock. I seem to have a herd of longhorn cattle that needs a home!"

"And it looks like, this time, I got all the good crayons," quipped Brandon.

YOU'RE READY FOR BOOK 11 in the *Justice Security* series: *Hell's Bells – A Justice Security Novel*.

It's available at your favorite eBook seller.

About The Author: T. M. Bilderback is a former radio announcer with a number of story ideas running around inside his head, most based on or inspired by classic songs. The author currently resides in Tennessee, and is writing feverishly in order to banish these stories from his head and into book form before he runs screaming into the street.

Other works by T. M. Bilderback

<u>N</u>icholas Turner
   If You Could Read My Mind
<u>Justice Security</u>
Mama Told Me Not To Come
Someone Saved My Life Tonight
Jackie Blue
Wake Me Up Before You Go-Go
Saturday In The Park
MacArthur Park
The Little Drummer Boy
The Night Chicago Died
Jim Dandy
Cow Patty
Hell's Bells
<u>Tales Of Sardis County</u>
Don't Come Around Here No More
Junior's Farm
The Devil's In The Details
I'm Your Boogie Man
<u>Colonel Abernathy's Tales</u>
The Lion Sleeps Tonight
Heart Of Glass
<u>Other Stories</u>
The Wreck Of The Edmund Fitzgerald
Gold
Hot Child In The City
Eli's Coming
<u>Other Novels</u>
Empty Eyes
<u>Story Collections</u>
Greatest Hits